COMPANION BRIEFING

Published by Pablo Star Media Ltd,
71 Shelton Street, London, WC2H 9JQ

Trevor J Willaims and Haydn Price hereby assert their so -called "moral rights of authors" in this work and any such rights under section 77 and section 80 of the British Copyright Designs and patents Act 1988.

First published 2017.

www.thespyacademy.org   www.thespyacademy.us   www.thespyacademy.ca

Pablo Star Media

ISBN 978-0-9956307-1-0

THE SPY ACADEMY®

COMPANION BRIEFING

The Spy Academy
Companion Guide

Contents

The Spy Academy – Companion Guide

Overview

The Spy Academy sees five perpetual teenagers working for a secret organisation trying to protect the world from the evil genius who gave them their immortality, Dr Ivan Zander. The five spies have special skills but their main power is their never aging permanent physical state.

Key points of The Spy Academy:

- The Spy Academy is unaffiliated to any government or organisation. The main characters are five Russian teenagers who took an Elixir during the Second world War and became immortal before escaping to America. They are not reinvented for changing time periods or decades, they have lived for around 100 years and this gives them a uniquely mature perspective with a teenage attitude relates to their primary audience. The teen audience are potential recruits into the Academy.

- The series offers us the chance to follow the teenagers through different periods of history starting with the 1920's and 1930's to the present day. Every story has some kind of historical context. The Spy Academy uses the last seventy years of world events to create its backdrop and offers a unique multi-generational theme.

- The Spy Academy cavern is beneath Manhattan and is a place of political neutrality where opposing espionage agents come together and learn new skills. Teenagers use hi-tech gadgets and enrol future generations to keep world stability. Mythical figures from spy fiction populate the organisation by way of affectionate analogues.

- Both the *good* and *evil* sides are defectors from the Soviet Union but the children were trained to infiltrate America so have developed and maintained American attitudes and personalities. This allows The Spy Academy storyline to

2

identify with a western viewpoint without allying with a specific nation or alienating other cultures. None of the major characters would accept a definition of themselves as "American" but see themselves as international citizens of the world.

- The mysterious and top secret Jynx Crystal technology that gives the characters their longevity is only a partially explained facet of The Spy Academy mythology. It is a useful tool for the creation of bold and colorful adversaries or fantastic situations (although it should not be relied upon to fill the brand. It is a brand about spies and espionage with the backdrop of modern political history upon which to play).

Each story should feature a flashback moment to some point in the Spy Academy's history. When the flashback scene/chapter occurs it should be simple enough to be informative for children and the younger audience with a few touches of nostalgic history for the parents and older audience. Not every tale need be all things to all people but as long as there exists a flashback in every story then there will be a consistent theme to the brand's fiction.

The flashback adventures should not heavily feature any guest analogues. We are not treading on the stories of older spies; they do not need the Spy Academy treading on their adventures just as we do not need their characters influencing ours. An affectionate and respectful tip of the hat is as far as we may go.

The technology level of the Spy Academy is key to its sustainability and must be very carefully measured. Writers must be careful not to strain credibility beyond breaking point. Audiences will accept only so many leaps before dismissing a product as "just for kids". When things go too far in, for instance, the James Bond films they must be reinvented. You can only limp along so long once you've included commercial space stations (the last Roger Moore Bonds) or giant orbiting laser cannons (the final Pierce Brosnan Bond) before you have to restart. The Spy Academy cannot be restarted; its history is a vital component of its appeal.

The already accepted leaps of faith are as follows;

- The Jynx Crystal and Elixir and its properties.
- Pegasus and his remarkable AI (since the sixties).
- Cyber Lady and her advanced robot shells.

These are enough of a strain for an audience. The introduction of anything as outlandish as time travel, aliens, magic or astral projection will not be allowed (unless it is a ruse as part of an espionage mission). Heroes

Heros

The Spy Academy heroes comprise a "teen team" of five immortal, enhanced individuals. Their physical aging was stopped in 1945 at the age of 18 and 19 by a formula known as the "Jynx Elixir" given to them by their mentor Doctor Ivan Zander. The team are youthful enough to feel the influence of their raging hormones and swings of mood but expirence gives them an appreciation and understanding people and thier deepest thoughts.

- Rebel: the undisputed leader. Cool but passionate, energetic and enthusiastic about the team's duty – to contain the evil actions of Ivan Zander.

- Rhona: the stoic lieutenant who hides her obvious love for Rebel until their mission allows them to stop the fight. Her contortionist abilities allow her to escape virtually any trap.

- Zack: the computer genius. Unashamedly geeky with an intimidating intellect. He designs devices in an afternoon that could make anybody a fortune.
- Gina: the undercover chameleon. She can impersonate anybody and with today's technology can appear as them too.

- Boomer: the trigger. The tortured youth whose only job seems to be to fire weapons when commanded to do so. His unerring accuracy is legendary. He carries a torch for the misunderstood girl on the opposite team, Kodie.

In addition to these main characters there is Pegasus, a sarcastic robot based on the personality of the teen's old handler, Chuck McCarthy, a rampantly patriotic company man.

The Spy Academy itself is a vast cavern beneath the streets, subways, and sewers of Manhattan Island, New York. There are several buildings in the central cavern and a network of interconnected rooms spreads under the city. It is an Academy with internationally selected espionage students can be found learning from the retired senior agents that help run the organisation.

The Spy Academy was founded during the Second World War with contractual donations secured from Britain, the US and many U.N. countries. It is kept secret from almost all politicians and the public at large.

Villains

The scope of the villains are such that they give a wide field of subjects for the spies to fight against; Organised crime (Kodie), Military dictatorship (Eagle), Technological terror (Cyber Lady), Theft and criminality (Boris) and scientific and corporate wrongdoing (Zander).

- Zander: the father figure to the entire Spy Academy brand. He invented the Elixir from the rare and otherworldly Jynx Crystal s. He tutored the teens and his own team members. He is head of an immensely powerful global corporation.

- Eagle: the monster. He used to be a military and assault specialist but is now a zombie. His colossal physique and unresponsive temperament make him an imposing figure. He is unaware of his cruel past.

- Kodie: the expert criminal. She used to be Zander's prodigy in the laboratory and now runs organised crime in New York, with operations in Vegas and LA.

- Boris: the skeletal thief with a ghoulish appearance who can crack any safe and enter any building.

- Cyber Lady: the robot with a psychotic personality. An unfeeling psychopathic woman with an endless supply of replacement bodies. The machine that hates humanity but is happy (for now) to execute only the ones Zander asks her to.

Zander's Elite operate out of Zander Tower, a commercial skyscraper in Manhattan. The Zander Foundation, a billion dollar organisation that runs thousands of companies and has a well-respected charitable division, is Zander's cover for most of his illegal activities. Zander has tried for decades to drill a path between his buildings cavernous basements and the Spy Academy main cavern.

Zander experiments on dozens of human subjects each year with variations of his Jynx Elixir. This creates enhanced individuals for the Spy Academy to fight or save. Zander chooses not to destroy the teens because they are the best results of Jynx augmentation he has ever produced. The psychosis that usually results from Jynx alteration has not affected them because of a strain of blue Crystal in their formula.

Ancient History

During the Second World War Franklin D. Roosevelt and Winston Churchill initiated the Spy Academy as an independent organisation to supervise espionage between nations in an effort to avert world wars. This has put them at odds with many contributing countries, particularly America.

The Manhattan cavern was carved out by 1945 and has been continually upgraded since. A rotating council of five senior spies from varying U.N. member countries has overseen the Academy's policy which has grown to include challenging corporate espionage, political corruption and the protection of international aid. In 1949 Kodie assumed full control of all organised crime in New York City. She remained an unknown figure, controlling from the shadows for thirty five years.

Chuck McCarthy, the U.S. liaison to the Spy Academy was a decent, honourable man who rarely let his intense patriotism interfere with his duty to the independent Spy Academy. His death in 1963 was a planned manoeuvre that included the creation of Pegasus the following year; a floating utility robot with McCarthy's acerbic personality. In 1966 during something that came to be known as the Nursery Standoff Boomer caused the death of Eagle, Zander's military specialist. Zander's experimentation caused Eagle's body to be revived in an obedient zombie-like state. It is unclear whether the thing controlling Eagle is his own brain or the Jynx Elixir that still runs through his veins.

There have been many instances over the years of Gina or a student of the Academy infiltrating either Zander's corporation or Kodie's criminal organisation. There have also been several instances of a member of the Academy being corrupted by one of Zander's team or a simple bribe. Neither side is able to relax their vigilance.

Zander thinks he is trying to benefit all of humanity with his Jynx experimentation and sees himself as the hero of the story (even though he would never release the secrets of the Jynx Crystal to anybody he did not control). The teen team search for a cure for their condition so they can bring down Zander for good, retire and start families of their own. Until then they will continue to recruit the world's finest teen agents to join the fight.

Public Name	Ivan Zander III
True Name	Doctor Ivan Zander
Occupation	CEO Zander Foundation, Scientist
Date of Birth	Unkinow
Apparent Age	45 (42)
Place of Birth	St Petersburg, Russia
Height	6 ft 1

Physical Appearance/Mannerisms

Ivan Zander is a slim man who wears make-up at public appearances to appear younger or older as appropriate. He moves and speaks with confidence and authority and has adopted an English accent over the decades.

Zander wears immaculately tailored suits that have stayed similar throughout the changing fashions of the twentieth century. Zander is an aristocratic, handsome, suave and gentle man who leaves physical tasks to others. Even his mannerisms while speaking are reserved and controlled; as though planned out in advance.

Zander's speech patterns and style of delivery have little variation. He will tend to give a compliment and an insult in the same commanding but neutral fashion. He uses humour on occasion, often with a self-deprecating style. Occasional flashes of frustration and psychosis come across as deeply threatening.

Zander remembers the thrill of being at Stalin's side at the height of his powers, and relishes the opportunity to command an empire and army of his own. The closest he comes to a genuine personal connection with another person is with Kodie who can share his thrill at the execution of a perfect plan.

Present Status

Ivan Zander III is the head of the Zander Foundation, a position he inherited from his father and his grandfather before him. He is known throughout the world as one of the wealthiest men on the planet and a beloved philanthropist.

He does not give interviews to the press and is seen as something of a bizarre recluse. This is widely believed to be because he was sheltered from the public gaze as a child. A cloistered, academic upbringing seems to have created a shy, enigmatic genius as determined as his father was to change the world for the better.

In reality he is the original Doctor Ivan Zander, kept alive by the miraculous effects of his creation; the Jynx elixir. Zander keeps his distance from the press in order to better keep this a secret. He allows none of his Elite team to appear with him in public. Kodie Ilyanov (the only Elite member with a human enough appearance to accompany him in public) is known to many of the New York criminal fraternity as the Boss of Bosses. Zander keeps his commercial, criminal and scientific worlds as separate as possible.

Zander uses the charitable arm of his multinational corporation as a cover to investigate possible sightings of Jynx Crystal s, the rare unearthly elements that Zander has developed into the Jynx Elixir.

Zander has developed a *truce of deniability* with the Spy Academy to keep the terrible powers of the Jynx Crystal s a secret. Each opposing side will cover up for the other to keep this formidable weapon secret from warring nations. Zander's discovery is a potential arms race to rival the atom bomb for destructive potential.

Ivan Zander is an extremely busy man not only because he runs a multinational business and charitable foundations alongside his scientific research but because he has many long term plans in operation at any time.

Behaviour

In order to engineer his own succession, to occupy the positions of his own apparent children, Zander must maintain strict routines. He must first suggest to the media that he has a young son being raised in seclusion. As his years must advance beyond his permanent apparent age of forty-two he must wear make-up in public appearances. When the "child" reaches thirty a look-alike actor is hired to make public appearances. When the child reaches mid-thirties Zander applies make-up to appear younger and takes his position. The public sham begins again.

The look-alike actors used in the past have been targeted for assassination when their jobs were finished.

Zander pays astronomers and archaeologists for regular updates on their work which he checks for possible discoveries of Jynx Crystal s. In the event that he cannot obtain a suspected sample by legitimate means he uses Boris to steal it, or Kodie to coerce its surrender.

Zander makes occasional forays into the entertainment industry. He will put a number of ideas into development, Spy stories in TV show format, or on film. He will pay for the best creative minds in the business to develop scripts and ideas for which they have signed non-disclosure contracts. From each of these ventures Zander has gained ideas on how to gain the upper hand with The Spy Academy.

Zander pays many corporate spies in companies all around the world to report on any advances in bio-chemistry, computing, robotics or weaponry. Some of these operatives realise, when the breakthrough they have reported upon is stolen, that they are largely responsible for the theft but these operatives are chosen for their greed and moral flexibility.

Whenever questioned on his motives for a villainous act Zander instantly draws upon the equation he constantly runs through his head, calculating the potential benefits to mankind of his Jynx Elixir against the criminal or unethical actions he takes. Unfortunately Zander views mankind with as much respect as he would a Petri dish.

Writer's Guide

Ivan Zander is the key antagonist in all the Spy Academy stories but need not appear in order to have his presence felt. Many villains tend to become impotent characters when their plans are constantly thwarted by the hero and it is vital this does not occur with Zander. Zander is a vital figure in the creation of the heroes and as such cannot be allowed to lose authority.

Although Zander's schemes cannot be allowed to succeed in full there should be some element of his plans in every story that he executes successfully. In a race to capture some artefact the teens should be successful but maybe leave the Academy cavern vulnerable to a theft by Boris. After a successful theft of documents from the Zander Foundation the team might discover that some traceable element led Zander to all the contacts visited in the adventure.

For each victory the team achieves Zander should always manage to claw back some measure of dignity, if not in valuable materials or information, then in pain caused to the teens.

The stories can involve matters unrelated to Ivan Zander but his century-plus of political manoeuvring and financial pressure mean there is little of consequence in this world with which he has not been connected. His presence in the story might be as little as a shadowed figure at the end of a phone line, or a signature on some significant document.

Zander is no *cackling maniac* driven by obsession; he has calculated the benefit to humanity of a refined Jynx Elixir and believes that his every action is in the population's (eventual) best interests. He still cares for the teens, as wayward as he believes them to be. He needs to keep them alive because they are the best example so far of a purely beneficial Elixir. The longer Zander lives the less he cares for human beings. He can see that generations can rise and fall (and have) while he searches for his perfect equations. The provision of political, criminal and financial control is something he sees as a necessary evil for him to complete his work.

Zander should not routinely be physical in his battles with the Spy Academy. He is a patient spider at the centre of his web, waiting for the perfect moment to order a strike. He is an expert swordsman and a fair pistol shot but likes to leave the mechanics of necessary violence to his Elite guard, or perhaps one of the many members of his private security force.

Zander does not tend to engage any enemy without at least two members of the Elite guard at his side, usually Kodie and Eagle. When Zander makes non-speaking public appearances it is usually performed by a double.

Zander does not shy away from committing terrible acts (including the disposal of subordinates in failed Jynx experiments, or virtual genocide for political ends) but can justify almost anything with the promise of eventually transforming the world with the Elixir.

The strongest trait of the character of Ivan Zander is his duplicity and cunning. As tragic as it would be for the character to become stale through over-use it would be far worse for his plans and schemes to become too simple; for the audience (at any age) to predict his every move. The brand of The Spy Academy has a unique opportunity to bridge a gap between children's and adult spy fiction. The vast backdrop of the twentieth century provides a huge arena from which to draw story ideas. While we should make every effort to ensure children can understand our stories it would alienate older readers for characters to be simplistic. If our fiction encourages children to question the motives of authority figures then we should not shy away from this. It is an inevitable bi-product of spy fiction.

Ivan Zander is, however much he might claim otherwise, a human being and as such fulfils a variety of roles in people's lives. While he is the essence of all the villainy in The Spy Academy universe he does not see himself as such and we should allow the audience the ability to believe in his self-deception.

Ancient History

Born in 1900 to aristocratic parents in Tsarist Russia, Ivan Zander was indulged by his adoring mother and ignored by an indifferent father. His father was an ageing military man, a captain in the Chevalier Guard. Zander's intelligence grew from a morbid curiosity. He would dissect small animals and experiment with chemicals and tissue samples in the estate cellars from the age of ten. All of the staff were told as a matter of policy to do as young Ivan asked, whatever his request. His experiments soon investigated the abuse of power.

In 1917, when the first of the revolutions came about Ivan Zander reinvented himself through the connections he had developed in the criminal underworld. He moved around the country to better observe the tumultuous events of that year and how best he could profit from them. In October, when Lenin and the Bolsheviks seized power, Zander positioned himself as a political supporter with tactical knowledge of use to the Soviets. As the Soviet government took shape Zander offered his already considerable scientific skills to Stalin himself; as an expert on poisons his knowledge would be called upon many times.

In 1928 Zander discovered he had an older half brother. His father had sacked one of the estate staff when she became pregnant with his child. The boy, Dmitri, grew up hating Ivan for his life of wealth and privilege. The October Revolution equalized their situations and ended the bitterness. Dmitri approached Ivan on a brief furlough from the Soviet Army. Ivan engineered an extended leave for the two men to get to know each other.

On a visit to an archaeological dig in Egypt in 1929 the two men discovered a glowing orange Crystal . Ivan demanded that their discovery be kept secret but Dmitri argued that they should present their discovery to the British for some wealth and luxury. Ivan knew that wealth and luxury would come eventually but was more patient than his brother. Only Ivan left the tomb. Zander still wakes up in a cold sweat remembering the terrible fate to which he condemned his brother.

Zander's experiments with his new discovery were many and varied. It's usefulness in munitions and chemistry were covered up by Zander who wished to study only their effects on biology; human biology to be precise.

Zander developed a serum less than a year after first discovering the Crystal. He tried it on animals, but began to fear the creatures and their potential, so had them terminated. He first tried an Elixir on a troubled, easily manipulated young laboratory assistant named Kodie. He named the solution the "Jynx" Elixir (based on ancient translations in Greek and Egyptian texts) and he was certain it would mean her death (if not from poisoning then from an autopsy). However, the compound had such a fascinating effect on the girl that she remains to this day a part of the Doctor's close group of advisors.

Zander developed the Elixir further over the next few years before presenting it to Stalin. He immediately appropriated the Elixir for his own needs, naming it the "Man of Steel" program after himself. Stalin was too paranoid, however, to take the Elixir before he had seen it tested on many other subjects.

Zander's project was first located in Leningrad at the Pavlovian institute but when it was besieged, the project relocated to the recently liberated Stalingrad. In that underground bunker Zander assembled a formidable team of patriotic orphans; Red, Rusna, Zacharov, Ginechka and Hammer. Zander had assumed the patronage of a special operations Spetsnaz soldier code-named Eagle, and had coerced the co-operation of a thief named Boris. Each was persuaded to take the Elixir. The beneficial effects convinced Zander to sample his own creation mere days before a Jynx Crystal was discovered with a vein of pure blue running through it. The elixirs made from this sample were given to the orphan group. It has given the most psychologically stable results of any sample of Elixir to date.

On the day of the orphans' defection to the West the defeat of the Axis was already secure. Zander realized that the division between the Soviet Union and America would be insurmountable, so he decided to take a stand. The USA gained a legacy of industry and fortune and Stalin lost his chance at immortality.

The Endless Fight

Zander did not face the teens as they fled Russia, he was busy tracking the progress of a meteor cloud which (he believed) contained blue Jynx Crystal s. Zander fled Stalingrad himself only days later, unwilling to be the one to explain to Stalin about the children's escape. There were a few other colleagues of Zander's in Russia who had taken some form of the Jynx Elixir but Zander only took with him those he felt he could trust or manipulate; Kodie, Eagle and Boris.

Zander's arrival in Manhattan was a well orchestrated affair. Kodie had already laundered money through various American banks from the sales of stolen Russian works of art and heirlooms. Her investments had grown into a company which had already purchased a skyscraper whose work on which had stopped when the war drives forced a halt on materials. The building would eventually become Zander Tower. The Spy Academy teens made their way to Manhattan shortly after Zander, and they had a deciding confrontation on the open boardroom floor of the partially constructed building. The battle lines were drawn and although Zander had not heard of The Spy Academy he bluffed that he knew all about it and it would not pose a threat to his plans.

Considering the political opposition he may possibly face, Zander decided to put into place several contingencies. He financed several terrorist groups around the world and promised continued funding as long as they enacted the "Zander Protocols". The same plans were given to several Jynx-altered agents from the Soviet military that waited undercover around the world. In the event of Zander's public death the agents were to try and contact him. Unless a certain coded response was given these agents would perform specific unspeakable atrocities around the world in order to secure their last piece of funding. This plan put a stop to any assassination plans, although the teens only found out about the protocols in the nick of time to stop an assassination attempt.

In 1951 Boris procured US military documents for Zander. Zander committed huge quantities of money and manpower to plans based on those reports. They turned out to be fake. In 1955 The Spy Academy's primary team spent four weeks in Moscow. Zander knew that their mission behind the Iron Curtain would ruin Boris's reputation in his home town but took advantage of the teens' absence instead and enacted other plans.

During 1956 Zander provided information to the CIA which he anticipated would draw a response from The Spy Academy. When Rhona took the bait and entered an embassy she found Zander waiting with an offer. He suggested ten-yearly summit meetings in order to arrange the continued covert status of Jynx technology, possibly surrender/swap sensitive materials and information. Rhona returned to the Academy convinced but spent the rest of the year arranging the first meeting so he could take no other advantage from it.

In 1960 Zander attended an auction at the Palace of Versailles for an artefact fashioned from Jynx Crystal . It was stolen before he could make payment and collect it.

Zander had an artificial agent created for his team in 1961, which evolved into Cyber Lady. In 1963 Zander lost a Cyber Machine model and nearly lost Eagle when Chuck McCarthy detonated an explosive trap. To Zander this setback was worth the elimination of McCarthy. In 1966 a repaired Cyber Lady contributed to the death of Eagle in *the Nursery Standoff* in Sweden. The Jynx-altered infants that the agents saw that day were apparently allowed to return home with their parents but Zander kept in touch with them and continues to monitor their growth and development of new skills. Later that year the Zander/Academy summit was held. Eagle did not attend.

In 1971 Kodie captured Gina who was undercover in Zander's organisation. Zander allowed Kodie to attempt brainwashing. Zander believes it was successful but has not tried to control Gina yet. He observes the self doubt and psychological trauma it causes her and simply watches for as long as it amuses him.

Later that year, 20 years after being fed bogus military documents by the teens, Zander returned the favour. His information led to a heavily armed expedition from the teen team in which Boomer was forced to take an innocent life.

Kodie was captured by the Soviets in 1973. Zander did not organise a rescue, instead enjoying direct control of the criminal underworld for six months. Kodie eventually returned.

In 1974, when Boomer appeared in Vietnam, Zander paid for several military intelligence agents to watch for his presence so he could operate more freely elsewhere. In 1976 another summit meeting was held.

During 1985 Zander learned that Gina was alone and unarmed in New Falls, surrounded by multinational agents. Seeing an opportunity to thin the ranks of international espionage agents and possibly blaming The Spy Academy, Zander assembled a terrorist task force to take them on. Gina could not save all the agents but was able to direct her colleagues, capture the terrorists and keep the Academy a secret.

In 1986 another summit meeting was held.

By 1994 Zander was able to capture the entire Spy Academy team at his Compound in Whistler, Canada. Zander could not contain his delight at such a victory. He teased Gina that she might yet be activated as his *sleeper agent*. He reminisced with Rebel about old times, and the obedience programming that Rebel still fought against. He thanked Rhona for her pacifist approach to their struggle, trying to imply to her team-mates that she might have been working for him. When he became bored he could not decide how best to deal with them, and certainly wanted them alive. He instructed Kodie to play on Boomer's expectations and allow him to escape and free his team-mates.

Then in 1997 another summit meeting was held.

In 1999 Rhona stole the parentage documents which apparently contained all the details of the teens' families. Only Rebel read the papers but then destroyed them. Zander falsified only a few of the details but Rebel's insecurity over the information's validity fills Zander with glee.

Zander's dalliances with women over the years have been trivial, functional relationships which have occasionally, accidentally provided him with genuine heirs.

The Future

Zander's brother Dmitri may have escaped the tomb and overcome the injuries and obstacles left by Ivan. This subject is one that haunts Zander and might be exploited by a foe who could get their hands on Dmitri's DNA. As far as Zander is aware nobody alive even knows that Dmitri existed.

There were several subjects who had taken some form of the Jynx Elixir in Russia before the defection. There have also been many subjects since then whose results have been questionable but have still survived. Any of these survivors might have good reason to seek revenge on Zander.

Zander has had a number of children during the twentieth century. Any of them might have inherited some portion of ability or immortality from his/her father.

The existence of Jynx Crystal Technology is not the only secret that Zander guards. His behind-the-scenes manipulation of political events has left his footprints across the twentieth century. There are many who would seek revenge if they knew the truth.

The criminal organisations of New York (the five families, the Yakuza, Crips, Bloods and others) have all felt the sting of Zander's leash around their necks. While Kodie is the visible face of control to the mob bosses, several of them suspect that Ivan Zander is the power behind her throne.

Within his own Elite Zander knows that Kodie's fragile psyche could shatter under such terrible stress. Boris has collected roomfuls of evidence with which he might one day try to barter his life back. Cyber Lady might one day circumvent her most fundamental programming and turn against her creator. Even Eagle might achieve more than just a spark of intelligence and personality one day; and if his wits return he would have many reasons to hate Zander.

The ongoing battle with the Spy Academy teens is a diverting game for Zander. Often he oversteps his own boundaries and worries that he might bring down the house of cards upon which their game is played. His obsession might drive him to lose his business empire, his public position and his team

Public Name	Eagle
True Name	*Unknown* Vitaliev
Occupation	Ex-USSR Army Captain, Spetsnaz* Operative
Date of Birth	**/**/1908
Apparent Age	31
Place of Birth	Siberia, Russia
Height	6 ft 2

Physical Appearance/Mannerisms

Prior to his death Eagle was a typically reserved military man. He remained silent for long periods breaking into shouts and commands when the situation demanded. His personal relationships were functional and cold, his personality sterile and obedient. An enormous and hugely developed muscleman, Eagle wore his Spetsnaz camouflage uniforms like a second skin. He enjoyed intimidating others with his stature and practising his various martial skills.

Eagle's death in 1966 cast a cracked ivory pallor over his skin. His muscles, once fluid and smooth now dragged beneath his dusty skin. His eyes, although still functional now seem like blank yellow sponges. Eagle can still move very fast but only when in pursuit of a goal. When motivated by Zander's commands he can still use martial arts and complex weaponry. The only emotion he conveys now is confusion or pain.

Present Status

Eagle acts as an obedient, characterless human robot. His personality still exists deep within his lobotomised shell, sleeping and simmering beneath the surface. It takes vast effort for him to venture independent movement or thought, making such events rare. Eagle still takes in all that occurs around him and can be affected by the actions and words of others although his behaviour rarely shows these effects.

Zander treats Eagle as a beloved Pet. He remembers and respects the relationship he had with Eagle before his death but sees the soldier only as a tool to further his own plans now that his conventional life has ended. It occurs to Zander only fleetingly that there might be a spark of independent life within Eagle. When Zander resurrected him he believed that he was bringing life only to the Jynx Elixir coursing through Eagle's veins, and believes to this day that it is the Elixir alone that animates him. If Zander sees any evidence or even a suggestion that Eagle's soul might still remain within his body he dismisses it as soon as possible. He secretly acknowledges that he may have been mistaken about Eagle's lack of life.

Kodie refuses to acknowledge the possibility that Eagle might still be alive. She is often (cruelly, she feels) sent out on missions with Eagle and treats him with contempt for the duration of their time together. Kodie sends Eagle on destructive, dangerous and possibly suicidal tasks as if testing his apparent invulnerability. She would be happy for Eagle to be eradicated as his zombie state causes her grief and confusion. She might go so far as to leave Eagle behind, if he could be actually destroyed. Rather than check for a corpse, she would rather leave Eagle to find his way home alone, despite the obvious security breach this would create. Eagle feels pain from Kodie's dismissals. Although over forty years have passed since his death and their relationship together, it still forms the basis of his memories of real life. Though he cannot express it he misses Kodie and the moments of intimacy they shared.

Eagle realises that he has an impressive power of intimidation over most people. It is something that has remained constant despite his death. What has changed is the level of intimidation he holds over Boomer. Eagle recognises and enjoys the effect his presence has on the teen agent.

Behaviour

Eagle rarely speaks. It is a huge struggle for him to think clearly let alone express himself so he chooses to remain silent most of the time. He follows orders without question, and will obey each command as literally as possible to the word. So Zander has learned to be careful in his choice of words. Eagle has no need for sleep. His mind is in a state of partial consciousness most of the time so he has no need of mental relaxation. Eagle does not feel hunger, so does not eat. His body still requires some nourishment but Zander gives this via a weekly injection of nutrient-rich fluid. Eagle does not seem to need to breathe. He appears able to hold his breath for days and can remain underwater without breathing apparatus. The need for oxygen in his bloodstream has been replaced by the unique activity of the Jynx Elixir.

However, he achieves moments of clarity when exhausted. The hours of inactivity he spends trying desperately to concentrate generally tend to achieve nothing. Eagle is far more likely to find his genuine personality rising to the surface when the Elixir within him has been pushed to its limits.

Eagle does not appear to be listening to conversations that occur in his presence but his memory operates in a very strange fashion. He can effectively memorise long periods of conversation but encounters difficulty in understanding or repeating them. His intelligence is very poor but he remains tactically alert and instinctual in combat situations. He can still operate complicated weapons and perform martial arts moves. He would be unable, however, to drive a vehicle or operate any computer based control system.

When not on a mission, Eagle simply sits in his bare quarters in the dark. There are still a few photographs on the wall (his first unit in the Cheka, his mother and sister) and some books by his bedside but they have remained untouched since his resurrection over forty years ago.

Writer's Guide

*Although the word Spetsnaz is used to describe Eagle's military career it is intended only as the "Special Operations" shorthand for secret, deniable missions. The official designation "Spetsnaz" was not applied to any unit until 1974. Prior to that point the word was unofficially used to describe a number of organisations including KGB, military and government groups. The first organisation in the USSR to use these tactics was the *Cheka* which initially recruited Eagle. The convoluted history of espionage in the USSR and Russia means we will use the word "Spetsnaz" as an umbrella for military espionage but writer's should be aware of its varied applications. Perversely the word *Chekist* is now commonly used to describe someone in support of militaristic/oppressive politics.

Eagle has many obvious uses as a character. At the present time he can be portrayed as an unstoppable juggernaut, a sad, simple soldier or a fountain of barely restrained rage. In flashbacks a writer can choose to contrast the current zombie character with the cool-tempered but eager sadist of his earlier life. There were over twenty years of direct conflict with the Spy Academy (1945-1966) to choose from in which Eagle was alert and intelligent.

Eagle can be used as an effective monster. His apparent inability (actually a refusal) to speak and intimidating physique make a formidable and seemingly unstoppable adversary. His ability to survive almost any punishment and repair his body back to its current state can be useful to explore inhospitable environments and create compelling settings for stories. Perhaps deep underground in near volcanic heat or even underwater, Eagle can persist with little protection or even any oxygen while the Spy Academy teens would need to maintain protective clothing.

When Zander made the decision to resurrect Eagle in 1966 the body had been clinically dead for six minutes. At that point in history it would have been acceptable to believe that there was no hope of continued life and so Zander changed his tactic from prolonging Eagle's life to exciting life within the particles of Jynx compound within Eagle's bloodstream. He was successful through a series of brutal electrical shocks while Eagle was suspended in an inert Jynx solution. The activity of the Jynx Elixir *has* brought back Eagle himself but only in a limited fashion.

The battle to express himself from behind the control of the Jynx Elixir makes Eagle a more sympathetic and therefore human character than he ever was in life. The professional ignorance he faces from his team-mates makes it all the more difficult to gain any confidence in his own existence. He lacks the tremendous strength of will to break free from the Elixir's control.

It may be the case that the Elixir has become detached from Eagle's nervous system and exists as a separate entity, effectively possessing him. This suggests a wealth of possible stories for the future. There could be such a thing as a dialogue of sorts between Eagle's human personality and his driving Jynx Elixir persona; perhaps using images rather than clumsy sentences. If such a story is pursued, however, it should be the beginning of a story arc with a conclusion in mind. Eagle is not a character that should be emotionally torn or conflicted – he is a terrifying powerhouse with tragic potential, not a soap-operatic, angst-ridden character.

Eagle's rather cruel and tragic back-story has possibilities for future stories. Eagle could easily be made to feel guilty if an incident reminds him of the fight to the death in the Siberian clearing. The blood of his neighbours on his hands was only the first in a long and bloody career. It also highlights that his inherent sadism was once the only means of escape from death for his family.

Eagle spent many years in various divisions of Stalin's military forces. He might have seen many things and know many secrets which his anguished and leaden brain would find hard to recall exactly. Brief flashes in Eagle's memory can be used as upsetting moments of character development, plot progression or laying clues for a mystery of some kind.

The most obviously tragic event in Eagle's life was his apparent death made all the more poignant by the fact that his relationship with Kodie (perverse and strange though it was) had become something more than a fling to them both. It is the depth of feeling Kodie felt at his death (and his horrific resurrection) that makes her act in such a callous fashion to Eagle today.

Ancient History

Eagle was born in a remote Siberian village in 1908. Life was cold, hard and desperate for him and his family. It is believed that his family name was Vitaliev but there is little evidence remaining to confirm this. He lived and worked with his family in a collective livestock farm that consistently failed to meet its targets.

In 1922 the farm was visited by a unit of Cheka soldiers who separated the men from the women and children. Eagle (nick named for his ability to spot prey while hunting) insisted he should accompany the men despite being only 14. The men were taken to a desolate clearing and told that there was one place available in their unit and the survivor would claim it. The survivor's family would be escorted back to comfort and stability while the farm was left to its own survival once the livestock was seized. Given that choice, Eagle managed to leave the clearing as the sole survivor. He could not bring himself to speak to the family he had saved and has not tried to contact them since.

After three years of training and eight years of action in Stalin's service, Eagle participated in the abduction and questioning of a young scientist who was about to work on a sensitive government project. He never met the subject face to face but was put in charge of the mission and observed the entire procedure from behind a glass screen where he admired the manic obsession in the girl. The young scientist was Kodie about to join the as yet un-named "Man of Steel" program.

Eagle met Ivan Zander three years later while on leave and struck up an immediate friendship. Zander asked a series of psychologically precise questions to judge Eagle's obedience to the State and general trustworthiness (two entirely separate issues). Eagle recognised that he was being tested and pointed this out to Zander. Zander immediately offered Eagle a place on his team, promising to arrange for Eagle's release from the Cheka if he agreed. Eagle examined Zander's operation and realised that Kodie was about to be the first recipient of Zander's new procedure. Eagle was to be Zander's protection if the test subject became violent. Already fixated on the young scientist Eagle agreed instantly, although his duties required him to be absent for the following few years.

In 1939 Eagle was given the Elixir and began to experience a massive increase in his strength and abilities. His employment offered him great opportunities to test his new abilities so he remained on loan to the

Cheka, meeting with Zander to report every three months. It was not until 1940 that Eagle met Kodie face to face. He has never revealed to her that he encountered her years earlier. Even Zander does not suspect that Eagle was a part of Kodie's abduction team in 1933. Later that year Zander was targeted for assassination by rivals for Stalin's political favours. Eagle stepped in front of Zander and took a bullet, proving the effectiveness of the Elixir at an early stage.

In 1942 Eagle spent 6 months in Stalingrad fighting the Nazis during the siege. His strength was still at an early stage of development but his resilience was put to the test as Eagle survived several assassination attempts. Eagle met the hero of the siege, Vasiliy Saitzev, while in the city and was disappointed at his lack of venom. Eagle abandoned the city and carved a path towards Zander through the advancing Nazis.

In 1943 Eagle was called to Stalingrad and told to report Zander once more. He came to the bunker to which the Pavlov Institute's project had been moved. Eagle was given the task of improving security at the bunker and training the military staff. While at the bunker Eagle was introduced to five teenagers in training to infiltrate the US. Eagle disliked the children but agreed to assist in their weapons and combat training. At Zander's request Eagle remained in the bunker for the duration of the project and has stayed at Zander's side ever since. In 1944 Boris was called to the bunker to assist in the youths' training. Eagle was asked to watch over Zander as he took the Jynx Elixir himself. Eagle was told to watch out for Boris as Zander still did not entirely trust the thief and worried about any state of incapacity. Eagle felt proud as he watched strength and confidence flood his mentor, and the Elixir enhanced his body. Eagle noticed a slight increase in Zander's paranoia and irritability but ignored it.

In 1945 the teens made their escape, defeating both Kodie and Eagle as they did so. On their return to the bunker Zander ordered their own defection. It was Eagle's final duty on Russian soil to clean out the bunker. He obediently burned out the rooms and executed the staff.

The Endless Fight

In 1945 Eagle contacted many colleagues from the military who left the USSR for mercenary work. These contacts gave Eagle the names of terrorist organisations and political despots with a need for funding and a willingness to commit atrocity. It was with these connections that Ivan Zander first established the Zander Protocols.

Eagle came to respect Rebel in 1953 when he was abducted by Zander's Elite and held captive. Under torture performed by Kodie and Boris, Rebel revealed nothing. Eagle did not, and will not, perform any torture beyond mental conditioning and is proud of his former student for his courage under duress.

In 1957 Eagle and Boris were set in competition with each other when they were given the task of assassinating one man. Eagle attempted a long-distance sniper shot, which failed, and a mortar attack on the mark's retreat. He survived to return to his bomb shelter hideout where Boris had been virtually hibernating for an entire week. Eagle was forced to settle his bet with Boris, but never spoke of the occasion again.

In 1958 Gina was captured in Las Vegas by Kodie. Eagle and the Elite were summoned to Vegas in anticipation of the Spy Academy's escape plan. Eagle was disappointed to learn that they were to let Gina's rescue succeed. He managed to fire a shot into McCarthy as he ran from their casino headquarters.

In 1959 Eagle initiated the assassinations of the three chief designers of the Spy Academy complex. He sent personal items of each of the victims to the Spy Academy base via a Post Office box. He imagined that the Spy Academy would worry that their structural plans had been compromised. In fact they knew that each of the designers was so obsessive that they had not shared their full plans even with the Academy Senior Council. Eagle's victory achieved nothing more than cheap cruelty.

In 1960 Eagle began a relationship with Kodie, a girl he had secretly desired since 1933. This new facet of Eagle's life made him a happier, more vibrant and decisive person.

In 1963 Eagle accompanied Zander's new Cyber Machine to intercept Chuck McCarthy with the notorious "Option 12" documents. On his capture McCarthy detonated an explosive device that destroyed Cyber Machine and nearly killed Eagle. It was this incident that led Zander to investigate methods of prolonging the life of a Jynx Elixir subject.

In 1966, on a mission to protect a nursery full of Elixir enhanced infants, Boomer caused the first death of Eagle. Though the bullets were fired by Cyber Lady it was clear that Boomer had caused the fatal deflection of gunfire.

In 1968 Gina attempted to infiltrate a low-level New York street gang with links to Zander. When Eagle accompanied Kodie on a routine inspection of her gangs it was Eagle who detected the presence of another Jynx altered subject in the vicinity. In the ensuing chaos Gina's confidant was killed.

Pegasus and Eagle met in 1978 under bizarre circumstances which to this day are not fully explained. Pegasus was running on a single, low-memory unit, Eagle was isolated from his back-up. They shared a conversation over a cup of coffee at a diner. Eagle only remembers the conversation in vague, brief flashes and Pegasus's recordings are so low-quality as to make their validity suspect.

In 1983 Rhona and Eagle became trapped in the rubble of an Ambassadorial residence in China. She talked to him, separated by feet of fallen masonry, unwilling to let him die. She coaxed a few moments of clarity from him and a few child-like sentences were spoken. Eagle cherishes this memory as one of the few moments of the last forty years when he has been treated as a human being by another.

By 1994 the entire Spy Academy team was captured in Zander Tower itself. Kodie was instructed to keep them all incarcerated until the entire team assembled, racing from around the globe. Kodie set Boomer loose to free his team, crying about the lost innocent personality she once showed to Boomer. Eagle was unaware that she was following Zander's orders but still allowed the escape. Boomer's cruel manipulation was Zander's only goal from the affair.

In 1998 Gina broke into Zander Tower and destroyed Eagle's quarters, hoping to eradicate the seemingly unstoppable thing in Zander's employ. It was Rhona who disabled the explosives believing (from her experience in 1983) that Eagle may be more useful alive than dead. She has always kept this a secret from Gina.

The Future

Eagle had many comrades in the USSR military that remained in contact with him in the years following the Elite's defection. Some of these men became mercenaries that were employed by Zander. Some of these men received Jynx treatments and are living in hiding waiting to enact their part of the Zander Protocols.

Eagle's struggle to reassert his personality over the controlling Elixir could be a very interesting and tragic arc. The Elixir itself might become effectively a second character inhabiting Eagle's body. Such a story should be limited and have an end in sight; Eagle is a tragic character but he was a sadist when he lived and must not be given too much sympathy. Eagle's existence as a slave to the Elixir could give him a greater sensitivity and instinctual knowledge of the Crystals. The ability to sense others who have been enhanced is more acute in Eagle but he has yet to display this talent to Zander.

Eagle's relationship with Kodie can also be explored for emotional impact on the pair. Flashbacks to 1960 - 1966 when they were an item contrast with later periods when Kodie has had other men in her life and Eagle has been unable to do anything but silently obey his orders.

The possibility that his condition might be replicated could be explored to great effect. This would be something that could spur Eagle to act independently. For Zander to try such a tactic he would have to find Jynx subjects with a long term dose and extreme levels of physical endurance then kill and resurrect them using the same methods. This would be a very costly tactic by Zander (and a very *long game*) but he might consider it worthwhile to create another obedient juggernaut. If asked by

Public Name	Kodie
True Name	Alexa Kodiniev Petrova
Occupation	Chemical/biological research Scientist and criminal kingpin
Date of Birth	XX/XX/1912
Apparent Age	23
Place of Birth	Unknown
Height	5'10"
Weight	Currently unknown

Kodie or Boris about failed experiments in this area he would explain that he was searching for a cure for Eagle's condition (if he bothered explaining at all).

In the event that Eagle should be cured of his condition in some future story it should mean a cure of Jynx enhancement altogether and ultimately death. Perhaps some redemptive action at the end of his life could be a part of the story but it would have to be the last Eagle story.

Physical Appearance/Mannerisms

Kodie is an intense, nervous and sultry character given to mood swings and personality shifts. She has an uncanny ability to bring about a fearful perspiration from anybody whose company she shares. A deeply troubled individual, Kodie uses excessive behaviour to bring herself attention.

Kodie is a tall girl (5'10 in her bare feet) but she likes to wear heels to at least equal if not tower over the men in her life. Like tragic and doomed "Jenny" in Forrest Gump (Robin Wright, below) her behaviour rocks wildly from one extreme to the other but it is, perhaps, more tragic that Kodie is technically immortal and doomed to continue her self-destructive actions forever. Paranoid and suspicious of everybody, Kodie is as likely to whisper as she is to yell. Unpredictable and terrifying Kodie does not take disappointment well, and has been known to kill messengers for the bad news they bring.

There should also be a sensitive side to her character (though not every story need feature it) and room for the audience to believe, along with Boomer, that Kodie's true nature is the gentle, encouraging soul he fell in love with in the Stalingrad bunker.

Present Status

Kodie is a stern leader of the criminal fraternity. She divides her time between this unique, challenging duty and obeying Zander like an eager puppy. Zander fills a father figure void in her life and she is devoted to him. Her personality switches from obedient pussycat to humourless control freak without a pause for breath.

Eagle's current state of zombie-level awareness is a constant torment for Kodie. She finds herself twitchy and unable to concentrate around him, and buries her personality in pure spite; she cruelly dismisses the hulking creature, refusing to accept that he might be the same man somewhere inside.

Kodie is suspicious of nearly everybody, even her closest comrades in Zander's Elite. She resents Cyber Lady even though her femininity is artificial. She is wary of Boris because of his sly nature; she believes he knows the truth about her personality disorders. She even suspects Eagle of faking his mindless status and sees any glimpse of intelligence not as a sign of hope but as proof of his duplicity.

Kodie has no respect for the teens because of their betrayal of Ivan Zander. She is privately envious of them for having taken the purest and strongest of the Jynx Crystal elixirs. She sees any subject of Jynx manipulation as uniquely blessed; even those for whom the dose proved fatal or mutative. Though her work with Zander has left a trail of bodies and broken lives through the decades she believes all who took the Elixir should be grateful to Zander.

There are always several long-term schemes bubbling away under Kodie's control. She has to spend a little time every day manipulating and checking on the many schemes in play.

Kodie has a separate personal fortune hidden away in a few international accounts. Some of it has come from insider trading and stock manipulation; some from theft.

Behaviour

Kodie has a number of routines she uses to keep her mental health under control.

She employs a computer program to surf through all CCTV data in which she appears. This program captures and erases the data from anybody else's systems, thus ensuring her activities are a mystery to the general public and to the criminal fraternity that obeys her commands.

Kodie actually performs this duty as much to review her own whereabouts on a day-to-day basis. Kodie cannot be sure, however, that her memories of reviewing the data are accurate but she cannot approach anybody else with such a sensitive problem.

In addition to this technical monitoring of her condition she undergoes therapy on a weekly basis under an assumed name and identity. She tries her best to disguise the details of her life as she has developed a bond with her therapist and would like to avoid killing her for as long as possible.

The management of her criminal empire has become much now that her true identity is widely known. She does not have to hide behind aliases to address her troops and her stern voice has become something to be feared. Kodie has weekly "board meetings" when she is in America and video conferences when abroad. She has a team of five subordinates whose job it is to manage the gangs in her absence. It is also a job for each of them to monitor one other of the five members and report back to Kodie.

Once every year Kodie calls a gathering of all the gang members. All high ranking members meet at a conference where strategic planning is put forward, where territories are divided and disputes are settled.

Some unofficial awards are given, along with a few booby prizes (beatings, executions) for poor behaviour.

It was at one such conference that Kodie's identity was revealed. She pretended she had intended to reveal herself for maximum impact to uncover sexism and bigotry in the industry. She dealt immediate punishments and gained further respect.

Writer's Guide

Kodie is a goldmine of a character on the villain's side. Her unpredictable nature can be used to inject a little black humour into a very dark subject. Her brilliance coupled with her unreliability can enliven a scene; she can perform bold, sweeping actions on a whim but has the intelligence to justify virtually anything she does. A sudden violent gesture in the middle of a calm speech can bring great impact to a scene (see "The Untouchables" *enthusiasms* scene) and can be all the more effective when Kodie falls back to a calm demeanour immediately afterwards. Kodie's fractured personality gives her the ability to lie with absolute authority. She can beat any lie-detector test.

Her resources are phenomenal. Rather than using the endless wealth of the Zander Foundation she can use the criminal network at her command to fulfil her wishes. Any use of the criminal fraternity in the story must include Kodie at some point. Boris has been excluded from his criminal society in Moscow because of a Spy Academy mission. The Academy has tried similar missions on Kodie but she has been tactically aware enough to foil them. When the teens did achieve a degree of success and revealed her true identity to the criminal underworld she managed to spin the result to look like it was her idea.

Kodie is skilled at computer hacking and sees Cyber Lady as a rival in this regard. While Cyber Lady is a computer intelligence, and therefore adept at the mechanics of computer crime, Kodie is more tactically gifted in the execution of a stray line of code here or a misquoted password there. Kodie can consistently invent new methods of mischief on the tool the internet has become.

Kodie constantly toys with the idea of torturing Boomer for his misguided infatuation with her. Many observers think she is so resolutely cruel because she so desperately wishes to believe that Boomer cannot be right about her. It is one of Kodie's deepest fears that in her heart she is a simple, gentle soul. Her desire to please Zander is so deeply ingrained in her nature that such a possibility would be terrifying to Kodie. She also feels responsible for classifying Zander's own Elixir as the best possible mixture weeks before the arrival of the blue-tinged Crystal s.

It would be inappropriate in our all-ages stories to show Kodie actually self-harming but she is certainly a candidate for such behaviour. She heals from virtually any injury so the scars would not last long.

Kodie's bizarre behaviour can actually be a handy writer's tool (though it should not become a crutch). If the plot of a story dictates that something should be done by one of the Elite but you have difficulty coming up with a justification for it, then she has a cast of secondary personalities to choose from who may have different motivations than the rest of the team.

The multiple personality disorder should not be obvious or blatantly exploited. It is something she has managed to keep hidden from the world for over seventy years and she should remain a respected figure in the criminal underworld. It should also be treated with care that it is not trivialised.

Kodie is a control freak of the worst kind, as likely to kill someone for spilling her coffee as attacking her. She is insanely protective of Zander and she suspects that he is aware of her personality disorder although this suspicion remains unspoken.

Be aware that if the personality disorder is to be used as a plot device it must be used consistently with credit to the intelligence of the audience. For another character to emerge from Kodie she must be alone and with an opportunity to cover her tracks after the event.

Kodie feels little guilt for any of her actions. Zander has given her advice ion justifying her terrible behaviour. If she were not the kingpin of the NY underworld then somebody else would be perpetrating even worse crimes. If it were not for her iron grip on the city's criminals, the destructive gang wars for turf would engulf innocents.

Ancient History

Kodie was born in 1912 into a large family. Her mother died giving birth to her so she was raised by a drunken father and her older sisters. The entire family was moved to a collective farm in 1920 and each of her siblings was sent elsewhere. As the last remaining child, Kodie's father became abusive and cruel to her. Missing her brothers and sisters, and needing protection, she developed alternate personalities into which she could retreat. In 1924 it was noticed by a tutor that she had a remarkable photographic memory. She was removed from her father's care and sent to Moscow where her academic education began.

In the following years of hard study and restful solitude her psychological troubles subsided. Kodie reached the age of 21 and took a break from the final year of her scientific studies to prepare for examinations. She was unheard of for eight weeks. She missed her examinations and had to have them rescheduled when she returned with a broken finger. Although her instructors were displeased they allowed her to finish her course and handed her over to the Soviet army for a career in military scientific research.

She met Doctor Ivan Zander in 1933 at the Pavlov Institute. He immediately recognised her potential and asked that she be transferred to his side for the "Man of Steel" project. She eagerly supported the suggestion but soon found a reason to regret it.

KGB agents broke into her room at 3 A.M. and dragged her to a sound-proofed room. She was questioned about her loyalty to the Soviet Republic, about the activities of her brothers and sisters and about the death of her father. He had been brutally murdered and buried in the collective earlier that year. Kodie pleaded under chemical and physical duress that she knew nothing about it and the KGB men were satisfied.

In her quarters, as Kodie wept for her father she suddenly remembered how she had broken her finger; fighting her father to the ground and burying him in the soil. Another personality assumed control of Kodie while she wept inside as her sanity cracked and crumbled.

Kodie developed a profound admiration for Zander who told her that he had arranged for the KGB agents who tortured her to be killed. She never discovered that Eagle was in charge of the team that day, watching the interrogation from behind a glass screen. Zander encouraged and moulded the young woman that Kodie was becoming. He welcomed her help in developing and refining the very first Jynx Elixir.

In 1936 after a number of partial successes with animal subjects, the pair faced a dilemma. If they gave the Elixir to a human subject they would either die in a horribly painful fashion or gain strength, skill and immortality. They felt that they could not risk losing a loyal friend, or risk empowering a prisoner or lunatic.

Kodie decided to end the indecision and broke into the laboratory one night. She took the Jynx Elixir, aged 23. She did not see that Zander's words had been suggesting this course of action and manoeuvring her into position. After a week of bed-ridden agony with Zander at her side (taking notes, detailing every step of the process) she recovered her strength and developed new abilities. Over the course of the next few years the Jynx Elixir was regarded as a partial success. The only drawback of the Elixir seemed to be a degree of mental instability which Zander was quick to blame on Kodie's childhood traumas.

Kodie assisted Zander in the creation of many more elixirs over the following years, including one for Boris in 1937 and one for Eagle in 1939. Kodie and Zander eventually agreed that they had perfected the Elixir in 1944 and after a few tests Zander took the serum himself.

Weeks later a new batch of Crystal was discovered with a vein of blue running through it. The pair refined a new batch of Elixir to give to the teen agents in the Stalingrad bunker. Early in 1945 the teens took the elixir, the results of which proved to outshine every previous mixture.

Zander has pursued blue Jynx Crystal s ever since, and Kodie has felt responsible for pushing Zander to take the Elixir too soon.

Kodie had developed an intimate connection with one of the young agents code-named "Hammer". She genuinely enjoyed his company and was able to dismiss the knowledge that the teens would soon be dissected for research purposes. When the teens escaped, she felt so betrayed that her feelings for the agent (now named "Boomer") soured into hatred.

The Endless Fight

On their arrival in Manhattan in 1945 (when the Soviets were technically allies with the US) Kodie spent the first few weeks under the instruction of Boris, learning about the structure of crime families and guilds. Kodie approached the takeover of the NY crime scene as a clinical experiment. It was initiated separately from Zander and his businesses and her success came as a welcome surprise to her mentor.

In 1949 Kodie assumed full power over the gangs of New York and all related mob activity. She has allowed other faces to pop up in the media from time to time to draw suspicion away from her own activities. Las Vegas, Chicago and the West Coast organisations all respected the boss of NY enough to stay away, even if they did not know her identity.

That same year Rebel and CIA agent Chuck McCarthy entered a Sicilian crime family. They worked undercover for six months learning as much as they could, finding contacts and evidence, sowing seeds of possibility for future infiltrations. Kodie was unaware at the time but has been trying to repair the damage done ever since.

In 1953 Kodie discovered Rebel contacting one of her operatives in Harlem. She captured the agent and brought him into Zander tower for questioning. She tortured and tested him before Zander found out and called a halt to it. He did not want his young test subjects damaged. While they debated his survival, Rebel managed to escape. He revealed nothing.

In 1958 Kodie captured Gina when she had been deep undercover for three months in Las Vegas. Kodie ordered Eagle to eliminate the family Gina had stayed with. Her torture techniques proved no more effective against a female adversary. Kodie developed a theory that the Jynx Elixir insulates the subject against the effects of torture. Zander suggested showing a faked classified document to Gina before her team arrived to free her. Kodie, as always, obeyed.

In 1960 Kodie finally began a long-postponed relationship with Eagle.

By 1962 Kodie arranged for the kidnap of five experts in the relatively new discipline of computing. For over a year she subjected them to an array of invasive and painful tests to create an artificial intelligence. In 1963 Eagle and Cyber Machine (the resulting crude AI) were nearly destroyed by Chuck McCarthy's final mission. When he detonated an explosive device that took his own life, he destroyed the robot and almost killed Eagle. Kodie felt terrible that she had taken the bait and approved the mission. During 1964 Kodie disappeared for six months. She reappeared claiming to have been captured by a terrorist organisation. This has never been verified.

In 1966 Boomer was responsible for the death of Eagle. That his corpse was resuscitated by Zander into an obedient zombie slave was unbearable to Kodie. In 1971 Kodie again captured Gina. Instead of torture Kodie attempted to brain-wash Gina. She believes she was successful but has not been allowed to test this theory. By 1973 Kodie was captured and interrogated for two months by the Soviets. She escaped alone. She discovered that the Elixir was no defence against torture. During 1984 Kodie's identity as boss of bosses in New York's underworld was revealed to her troops by The Spy Academy in the hope of damaging her position. She manages to twist circumstances to make it look as though it was all her idea.

Kodie captured whole team in 94 and was eager to try her brain-washing techniques on all of them. She was ordered instead to release Boomer who then released the others. She has wondered if Zander gives such orders to thwart her wishes and solidify his position as leader. It has since been revealed to her that Boomer's infatuation of her had been waning (partially due to Kodie's increasingly cold and brutal behaviour, partially due to another woman in Boomer's life). Zander knew that this gesture from Kodie would ruin Boomer's personal life and re-establish for the teens the idea that Kodie may be a good person at heart.

Kodie has, through careful investment and occasional violence, influenced the boom in home computing and the internet. She has abilities in this regard that few people could imagine.

The Future

Kodie's past relationships are fertile ground for stories;

Zander might push her too far and become a genuine father figure to her (remember what she did to her real father – see Ancient History). Eagle might regain some semblance of memory or personality and bring chaos to Kodie's mental state. Boomer's own devotion to Kodie (or to some aspect of her personality) could bring about disaster in so many ways. She could begin to believe his notion about her true self being kind and gentle, she could rebel against it or she could manipulate Boomer in some cruel fashion.

Kodie murdered, manipulated and maimed her way to the top of the Big Apple's crime structure. There are many lifetime's worth of vendettas waiting to play out. Kodie had an unspecified number of older brothers and sisters. There could be plenty of Kodie's grand-nieces and nephews waiting to call on her. Her enemies might discover this and use the information against her.

Kodie killed her father while under the control of a distinct and separate personality. This may not have been the first or last time it happened. A separate personality may lead her into a trap in order to assume dominance (it has happened before in Afghanistan). Kodie believes that she has kept it a secret that she has multiple personality disorder. In her position of power several personalities could be running different schemes and plots against each other.

Kodie was the very first subject to receive a dose of the Jynx Elixir. There may be some long term side-effect to the dose and it would affect Kodie first. Zander would want to perform tests that Kodie would find objectionable.

This or any number of other factors may cause Kodie to rebel against Ivan Zander.

Public Name   Boris Smith
True Name   Boris Andropov AKA Boris Greschenko AKA
                       Boris Lienkovich
Occupation   Acquisitions Specialist
Date of Birth   **/**/1902
Apparent Age   38
Place of Birth   Moscow, Russia

Physical Appearance/Mannerisms

Boris is tall, bald and painfully thin. He tends to smother his stretched frame with heavy overcoats, scarves and baggy clothing. His eyes are sunken and shadowed. Boris has a wide mouth occasionally stretching to a leering grin. He has Cyrillic symbols tattooed on his left arm and a scar running diagonally across his back that does not heal.

Boris moves slowly but with grace and complete silence when he so wishes. Boris's beady eyes twitch and dart with a manic intensity. He licks his lips when he concentrates but rarely sweats. Boris prefers to remain silent and listen in most conversations.

Boris has immensely powerful hands with grotesquely swollen knuckles on his fingers which he can pull straight and slender when the situation requires it. The hands are usually gloved with specially tailored black leather.

Boris is twitchy and paranoid when unexpected events happen. Always mentally preparing an escape route or examining the contents of a room for its most valuable items Boris is never content or restful.

Present Status

Boris is the world's premier thief and cat-burglar and he is well aware of the title. His nearest challenger to the position is Rhona of The Spy Academy team but she rarely beats him to a target.
Boris has not been to his home town of Moscow for over fifty years without a disguise such is the level of disgrace put upon him by the Spy Academy in their 1955 mission. Though discredited in Moscow the

Muscovites do not repeat his supposed crimes. To speak his name is to risk a blacklisting by the black marketers and so he maintains a level of mystery and prestige in the world's criminal communities.

Boris trusts no-one. He feigns trusting obedience to Zander but Zander is aware of his doubtful allegiance. Boris feels pity for Kodie and her tortured mental state, more pity than Zander feels for his obedient pet. Boris misses the antagonistic relationship he had with Eagle. Boris has a superhuman grip in his large, dextrous fingers. He is able to control his own heart rate, breathing and even temperature to an extent.

Of the teens in the Spy Academy Boris feels a grudging affection for Gina but contempt for all the others. Gina showed a level of fortitude and determination that impressed Boris in the Stalingrad bunker and her persistence since has only improved his opinion. Boris does not care about the supposed rivalry between him and Rhona; he is certain of his own dominance in the arena of theft and duplicity.

Boris currently has active warrants for his arrest in 42 separate countries. He has only had to use Zander's influence to ensure his release on three occasions and has been forced to show gratitude on each occasion. This is enough incentive to keep Boris on his toes when performing any of the various illegal services he provides for Zander and other paying customers.

Boris performs independent jobs for external clients when his schedule of work for Zander allows. This work has included corporate theft from the Zander Foundation which Boris has managed to keep a secret. Boris enjoys testing the limits of trust in his relationship with Zander.

Behaviour

Boris practises his stealth and burglary skills on floor 101 of Zander Tower which is fitted out to his exact specifications. There are traps to escape, leaps and dives to perform and sensors to trick. The floor remains undiscovered by any staff working in the building because it has no doors. The only way to enter the floor is to break in through plumbing or ventilation systems or structural defects.

Boris maintains detailed diaries of the conversations he overhears between the powerful individuals he meets. This was a practice he began on his release from the Lubyanka Prison in 1926. He realised while meditating in his cell that he had been betrayed by the gang leader and vowed never to allow such a thing to occur again. Boris has many times felt compelled to threaten Zander with the release of his diaries but has not yet revealed this traitorous threat Zander.

Boris talks to Kodie with a friendly, patient tone. He taught her most of her skills in running the criminal empire of New York and has always felt pity for her fragile mind and splintered personality.

Boris dislikes being given orders with little notice. He has always stressed to Zander that his particular skills are best utilised within a plan with as many variables calculated as possible. When Zander orders an immediate response from Boris he is warned that he will not be getting the best use of his resources. Boris believes that Zander sometimes creates emergency situations to test Boris's loyalty under pressure.

When given time to prepare for a mission Boris will perfect a complex package of plans. If given enough time he will often add another layer to the mission to bring some benefit directly to himself.

When Boris is given a mission at short notice he immediately looks for some aspect of business that Zander might want to hide from him. Twice he has discovered that his mission for Zander would have a negative impact on his own professional standing or some of his colleagues outside of the Elite. In both instances he has been able to develop counter missions to nullify these ill-effects.

Writer's Guide

Boris is one of the main five villains of the Spy Academy world. One of Zander's Elite Guard since the thirties, their long relationship does not translate into trust. Boris is something of a counterpoint to Chuck McCarthy in that Chuck represented the best that capitalism had to offer: self-reliance, determination, resilience and freedom to choose, while Boris represented the worst: greed, possessiveness and a narcissistic self-absorption.

Boris might be lined up on the baddies' side but he is only looking after the interests of one man – himself. That being said he is also the most likely villain to help the Spy Academy team as he owes little or no allegiance to Zander. If the story dictates that somebody on Zander's team must help the teens (and a suitable justification can be found) then Boris will happily be the one to betray his comrades.

The idea that Boris is the likeliest candidate for betrayal must be handled very delicately if used. Zander is a proud man who will not stomach betrayal. If he perceives a genuine double-cross then he will make every attempt to kill Boris. The perception of the Spy Academy that Boris might leave Zander's team is a far more useful tool than actually having it happen (and thereby ending the character's effectiveness). It is also an exciting idea to have Boris placed in situations where he has difficulty deciding which side of the fight to play on. He must, however, always choose (or appear to have chosen) Zander's Elite.

These stories can be very hard to write while including the entire audience but can be very rewarding when successful. In such complex stories it would be a far better idea to concentrate on just him, Gina and Zander, with the other characters supporting.

Boris is a very proud man when it comes to his abilities. He will accept any challenge to prove himself the better burglar, safe-cracker or pick-pocket. His sense of self-preservation is so strong that were he captured in a pair of handcuffs he knows that he would lose a hand rather than face a lifetime (or more) in prison.

Boris should remain a character in the background for most stories. His desire to shrink into the shadows means he is rarely the focus of a scene. If he is to be featured in a story it must be remembered to keep him a spooky and enigmatic character. It would be easy to allow him to appear foolish (bald, skinny guy with bug-eyes and big hands) rather than creepy (scarred waif-like recluse with spider-thin limbs and intense stare).

Boris does not routinely use his powerful grip in violence but he will not shy away from such action. It is only that Eagle is such an obvious powerhouse that to show Boris's grip in combat might steal his comrade's thunder.

Boris is the closest thing Zander has to an equal on his team and Zander should be shown to occasionally give an order or make a comment to undermine Boris slightly within the team. Zander is petty enough to feel threatened by Boris's independent nature and cruel enough to crush it whenever possible.

Boris does not have romantic relationships with anybody. He occasionally takes a woman as his partner but he has only ever enjoyed relationships when he was pulling a confidence trick on a woman. The sensation of being "in character" is far more comfortable for him than natural interaction.

It is true that in modern times one can steal far more money with a computer than with a glass-cutter but Boris has never enjoyed pursuing mere money. A priceless and fragile artefact is far more appealing to Boris. He enjoys the challenge far more than the acquisition.

Ancient History

Boris Andropov was born in 1902 to a comfortably wealthy family. His father was a master watchmaker who schooled his children in the intricate craft. He told the youngsters that their hands would make their fortunes and gave the family a luxurious lifestyle when the Tsar Nicholas commissioned a series of elaborate clocks and pocket watches. When the second revolution came in October 1917 Boris's father was dragged from his shop and hung for his affiliation with the royal family.

The fifteen-yr-old Boris moved his mother and sisters to another part of the Moscow suburbs where they settled under the name Greschenko while Boris paid for their upkeep with burglary and petty theft. Boris was noticed by a Guild Master, Poliakov, on the streets of Moscow and brought into a gang where his skills were encouraged and honed.

The years of practising intricate watch assembly had given Boris a skill and dexterity beyond any of his rivals and he soon rose to be second-in-command of the criminal gang. Under the apprenticeship of the thieves guild, Boris developed a sparse diet which he keeps to this day to maintain a strong but skinny physique.

Boris managed to put together a permanent line of credit for his family in Moscow's black market. He visited them less and less as his criminal skills developed, initially reluctant to allow them into his new, dark world but later because his exploits allowed for little outside interest.

In 1923 Boris was arrested and imprisoned by the Cheka (the early KGB). He was put in the Lubyanka prison, a basement level of cells beneath the headquarters of the Cheka. During his time in Lubyanka Boris was beaten and tortured in an attempt to gain information about the Moscow black market. Boris revealed nothing although the abuse left a diagonal scar across his back where the whip regularly dragged a path through his skin. His prison details were tattooed on his left arm.

Boris was released in 1926 in an attempt to track his movements. While his release was processed he memorised the parts of the Lubyanka through which he was led. Boris, who had been performing mental and physical exercises in his cell every day of his sentence, disappeared from the surveillance of five experienced Cheka agents. He met up with, and assumed control of his old gang. He chained Poliakov in a basement and instructed the gang to construct a courtroom while he obtained evidence.

Boris broke in to the Lubyanka less than two days after his release and found the evidence to prove what he had suspected. He managed to escape without raising an alarm, destroying any evidence of his own existence in the process.

When he returned to the gang Boris showed the men evidence that Poliakov had been working with the Cheka, supplying goods and sacrificing men to their judicial system when required. Boris allowed the court to decide Poliakov's fate but did not stay to watch the execution.

In 1931 Boris took a personal contract which was to change his life forever. The employer was anonymous and the victim a little known young research scientist in a branch of the Russian Government. The scientist was Doctor Ivan Zander who hid waiting in his study for twenty hours for Boris to make his move. Boris negotiated with Zander at gunpoint. Zander told him that his employer was already dead and the only way to avoid execution was to agree to work for him. Boris accepted, never knowing but always suspecting that Zander had been the *deceased* employer all along.

Over the next decade Boris earned more of Zander's trust and began to seek out suspected Jynx Crystal s across the world. He met Eagle in 1935 and was told about Kodie in 1937. He learned all about the Jynx Elixir and although he had no great desire to take it, he saw no great harm. Kodie certainly seemed affected by paranoia since the dose but to a thief paranoia is an effective tool, he reasoned. Eagle took the Elixir early in 1940 and six months later Boris followed him.

Boris assisted Zander in the Pavlov institute and later the Stalingrad bunker where he familiarised himself with Western culture and language. Realising that his name "Andropov" might describe a punishment for theft in certain Middle Eastern countries he decided it would be tempting fate to resume it. Boris went by a variety of non-descript surnames in his final years in Russia.

The Endless Fight

Boris had spent little time with the teens before their departure, despising children in general. He found Gina's mock shyness intriguing and had begun to instruct her in all forms of deception. Rhona's more obvious skills were, Boris believed, stifled by her honesty. When Boris arrived in New York he was overjoyed at the differences. In Moscow one had to lie to be accepted by the state and its draconian laws. In New York the state ensured a man's freedom to lie as much as he wanted.

Infiltrating many levels of society, Boris learned the similarities between the two cultures and was able to instruct Kodie in her take-over of criminal culture. Boris taught Kodie all she needed to know to rule the gangs of New York with unquestioned authority.

In 1951 Boris was personally instructed by Ivan Zander to steal some military documents. Boris was able to procure the documents with little effort and supplied them to Zander. The documents proved to be faked, inspiring a costly and embarrassing manoeuvre from Zander. Boris suffered Zander's wrath over the incident and kept quiet his opinion that the decision to go after the documents without confirming the source was a stupid idea. Instead he decided to assemble incriminating information on Ivan Zander to better enable him to plead his case. As he had done for each of his superiors Boris began to find out exactly where Zander's bodies were buried. The diaries are still being kept today.

In 1953 Rebel was abducted by Zander's Elite and held captive. Under torture performed by Kodie and Boris, Rebel revealed nothing. Boris used the opportunity to study Kodie as much as Rebel. Boris did not enjoy such a gruesome task but appreciated the chance to see his team-mate's psychosis in full force.

In 1954 Boris began instructing a class of juvenile pick-pockets and cat-burglars in Hell's Kitchen in New York. One month into the class Boris spotted a heavily disguised Gina almost immediately. He allowed the lessons to continue, suggesting more and more that he knew her identity, watching for the moment when she would cut and run. It would be three months before she left his tutelage. He was proud of her audacity and never told Zander.

In 1955 Boris stole property from Chuck McCarthy's family home. In retaliation McCarthy designed an undercover mission to Moscow where Boris's reputation amongst the criminal underworld was ruined. Gina and Rebel planted evidence and spread rumours that Boris was originally responsible for the Cheka collaboration of which he had accused Poliakov (the former gang leader). The team arranged for relocation of Boris's surviving family members to a place even Boris could not discover. Boris felt for the first time the kind of fury Zander felt towards the teens.

In 1957 Eagle and Boris were once given the task of assassinating one man but for now his identity is still classified. Eagle attempted a long-distance sniper shot which failed, and a mortar attack on the mark's retreat. The mark survived to return to his bomb shelter hideout where Boris had been virtually hibernating for an entire week. Eagle was forced to settle his bet with Boris, but never spoke of the occasion again. Sensibly realising it would be best not to antagonise Eagle, neither did Boris.

Boris planted bogus information in 1971 to force a mission from the Spy Academy. It had been planned for over three years and executed with such precision that even Zack had no doubt of the situation. Boomer had to fire a shot intended to incapacitate but which triggered a security device bringing about the death of an innocent. This was clear revenge for the damage done to Boris's reputation and the removal of his family from Moscow.

The "Blackmail Contract" that Zack decoded in 1975 was Boris's work. He has still not claimed responsibility for the article which brought chaos to businesses and governments for three months.

In 1980 Boris first found a way into the Spy Academy main cavern undetected. He used the same entrance twice more in the same decade but has also used double agents to plant evidence of many more incursions. The knowledge that the Spy Academy must doubt its own security gave Boris immense satisfaction. This feeling peaked in 1989 when they installed a system of internal offensive weaponry designed to track and subdue intruders. Cyber Lady was able to hack into the Academy's computer systems and use the weapons against Academy personnel. Boris's glee was unrestrained for weeks following.

During 1998 Boris surprised Boomer with his ability to snatch one of his sharpened boomerang blades from the air. A re-design was forced upon the entire range.

Boris enjoyed his walk to freedom from the NY courts in 2002. He spoke of a travesty of justice while on the witness stand, all the while staring at Rebel. Although this was the third time that Boris had needed legal help from Zander he was still able to enjoy a small victory. As he left a free man he childishly bumped into Rebel, leaving a hand-written note deep within Rebel's wallet. The note read "Faith in the system? Easiest theft I ever made."

The Future

Boris has made many enemies and been many things to many people in his life. The possibilities for an element of his past returning to confront him are very wide.

For the first fifteen years of his life he was a dedicated student in Tsarist Russia. He has family (he lost track of them in 1955) and friends who might still survive if they came into contact with Zander and his work. The men who murdered his father and made their own use of the October revolution could have been kept alive somehow (Jynx Elixir, Cryogenics or just inspired a group of modern day thugs).

The members of his gang (particularly Poliakov, whose execution he *did not* witness) would have reason to track him down given his despised reputation following the 1955 slander assignment.

The people from whom Boris has stolen count among the richest and most powerful in the world. They or their children could arrange for all sorts of problems. Of particular interest would be a corporate war sparked between some Bill Gates-alike who was robbed by Boris and Zander who shelters him. Boris has also conned the rich and famous out of more than just possessions.

Boris plans for very long games of confidence. A story could start out as something straightforward but end up as a complicated con to benefit Boris. The possibility that Boris might aid the Spy Academy or seek *their* aid someday might go well with this idea.

Boris has taught classes from time to time. An old student of his might come to him seeking his aid or with a proposition for a job. There would, of course, be more to their story than first appears.

The diaries Boris keeps are potential disasters for the character. If he were to lose a diary, or even one page, he would become even more paranoid than normal. Who would have taken it and why? Have they read it and who will they tell? If Zander were to find those diaries it would be Boris's last story.

Public Name   Cyber Lady
True Name   CYBER LADY 7.8 cxvii-jlp
Occupation   Technical Expert
Date of Birth   N/A
Apparent Age   25
Place of Birth   Zander Tower, Manhattan, NY
Height   6 ft

Physical Appearance/Mannerisms

Cyber Lady is an artificial intelligence inhabiting a host body; a mechanical shell designed for a specific purpose. Her exact appearance depends upon the mission she is performing at the time but she has a *default* appearance as follows. She wears a head of long dark hair, full enough to hide wires and access ports (USBs) at the back of her head. Her lips are full and soft, her eyes wide and dark. She wears a lifelike sheath of fake skin over her regular robotic shell but chooses to have panels of bullet-proof plastic glass exposing circuitry and gears beneath. These panels can appear in varying places according to the effect Cyber Lady desires her unveiling to provoke. Her silhouette is routinely that of a tall, voluptuous and sexy woman.

Cyber Lady can wear shells sculpted to imitate actual people and her programming can exactly replicate their behavioural patterns; their speech, movement and mannerisms. However Cyber Lady despises humanity and organic life in general with such a passion that she seldom accepts such missions. Only a skilful and experienced observer can detect the repetitive, automated fashion of Cyber Lady's mimicry. Cyber Lady is generally distrustful of everybody and holds herself in a haughty and disdainful fashion. She appears statuesque at almost all times due to her having few typically human weaknesses. She can appear to be out of breath, her full chest heaving beneath her clothes but she does not breathe, nor sweat, and if her breasts are moving then it is all intentional.

Present Status

Cyber Lady is now using operating system v7.6, a faster method upgraded from the last to include better appreciation of subtleties like humour and cruelty. Each upgrade serves to make Cyber Lady's personality harder to distinguish from a regular human which would seem to indicate an intent to emulate humanity. Cyber Lady would argue that this is not the case. She only wishes to have the skills and ability to manipulate and fool humans, she does not wish to be like them at all times.

Cyber Lady obeys Zander not out of loyalty or gratitude for the money and resources he provides to maintain her hi-tech existence but because she fears that her programming may be compromised. She worries that there may be lines of code embedded in her personality construction that force obedience. She has other resources, however, and can access them when necessary to appraise her situation. She has a contact in Detroit that she meets by activating a drone body at the same time she occupies a primary unit. Although the practice is exhausting and difficult, Cyber Lady feels it is necessary to keep her other resources secret from Zander.

The Zander Foundation employs its considerable resources tracking the latest developments in computing and robotics. Using a vast network of independent companies Zander is able to keep Cyber Lady's technology years ahead of anything on the market or even to governments or the military.

Cyber Lady favours the dependable weapons of the extendable blade in one arm and a concealed firearm in the other. Although technology has advanced to offer many alternatives she finds these the most reliable and has settled into a level of familiarity with their use.

Behaviour

Cyber Lady has a phenomenally good memory, able to recall at a moment's notice any scrap of data from the powerful memory banks constantly running in the basements below Zander Tower. There are several subterranean compounds in North America and one in Austria where similar floors of computers store memory data. Cyber Lady routinely drops certain articles of information that have not been accessed for a significant period of time, confident that a hard copy of the data still exists at one of these repositories. This makes Cyber Lady very wary about discussing her memory capabilities, however. While she is happy to harp on for hours about the obvious dominance machine intelligence has over biological entities she is perpetually nervous about the fact that there seems to be a plane of existence (be it mental or spiritual) that biological beings can access that technological beings cannot. She is tied to her physical memory repositories and it causes her anguish to accept this.

Cyber Lady treats everybody with contempt, ally and enemy alike. The only entity in existence to whom she might show decency is Pegasus because it is biology that she despises. Pegasus, however, is despised because of the deference and respect he shows to human beings in general and Chuck McCarthy's family in particular. Cyber Lady acknowledges the four human computer scientists who gave their lives so that their personalities might be effectively recorded onto her personality matrix, but refuses to be indebted to them. It has been suggested to her by Boris that her hatred of the biological only comes about because her dominant personality is based on that of Francesca Franzia, a famously paranoid woman subject to bouts of self-loathing and destructive abuse.

The expansion of the Internet and wireless computer communications in particular has brought an exponential explosion in Cyber Lady's capabilities. In the past when she has needed to perform some computer or internet task she has needed to be connected to a mainframe or even in standby mode while her processors execute the program. In recent times her technology has been able not only to perform the actions simultaneously but also to connect to the Internet from virtually anywhere. The world's desire for convenience has enabled one of the world's most terrifying criminals.

Writer's Guide

Cyber Lady is an unashamedly evil villain. She has motivations legitimate to herself but as they only favour artificial life over biology it would be strange for the audience to sympathise with her. She despises humanity for its affectation and hypocrisy and is proudly cruel given the opportunity.

Cyber Lady makes herself look attractive as a distraction to and also a comment on male humans. Her silhouette is almost always that of a curvaceous lady but she chooses to wear transparent panels that let the light shine past her moving gears and LEDs. Her silhouette can become sinister with the right amount of detail.

The ability to wear virtually any shape to house her intellect makes Cyber Lady a tempting figure for infiltration but her personality has a violent dislike for pretending to be human. Her default appearance is considered her *true identity*. Similarly while she *can* secrete gadgets and weapons from inside her robotic form it is not something she should do regularly; that is Pegasus's trick. Cyber Lady has two regular hidden weapons; the blade-arm and the gun-arm and it would be acceptable to produce one additional item from her bodywork per story but only if necessary and hopefully in some elegant fashion.

Cyber Lady's character is paranoid, secretive and vicious but she does not sneer, scowl or show her emotions openly. While she has machinery designed to emulate emotional responses she likes to keep a calm, dignified, icy façade up at all times and, as she does not need to move or breathe, she is spectacularly good at this. Her ability to remain still could be used to good effect in stories, e.g. A female nude marble statue in a museum or lobby turns out to be Cyber Lady waiting for the moment to strike; playing dead on a battlefield while the victorious enemy approaches turns the tables for the Elite (Eagle could also join in on this one); Cyber Lady could act normally in a poison environment and invite victims to come and join her.

An intelligence such as Cyber Lady could occupy multiple bodies at once but that is a very intellectual threat rather than a personal conflict. It would be better to keep Cyber Lady in one body (or at least one at a time) in order to better develop the character. She can certainly be accompanied by a squad of shell bodies acting on some kind of drone program like soldier ants obeying the queen. If Cyber Lady were then to be destroyed her consciousness would simply animate the next available drone.

Cyber Lady's spiteful character comes from the inspiration of the abducted and executed computer experts but it should be remembered that Cyber Lady is not a human trapped in a robotic shell. It is enough of a torture for Cyber Lady that her opinions and behaviour have been influenced by a human. She can certainly be tormented by flashes of human experience and perhaps be motivated to eliminate reminders of her hosts' lives. Perhaps she might pursue and try to eliminate the families of the hosts in addition to a Zander-ordered mission.

Cyber Lady observes all the interpersonal relationships at work in both Zander's Elite and the Spy Academy teen team but she is no expert. She can see the basic themes in action such as the scorn and longing between Kodie and Boomer, or the respect, hatred and disappointment between Rebel and Zander but she cannot appreciate the deeper levels of connection between them and refuses to accept their existence. Romantic love, for example, is a product of human fiction in her opinion (and she will refer to ancient texts to support her claim – as if desperate to deny the thing she cannot appreciate).

It would be unwise to let a story get into any deep philosophical debates about emotion and humanity. Star Trek is the place for rants about "the special-ness of humanity", not the Spy Academy. The teen team have seen too much inhumanity over the decades to offer much resistance to Cyber Lady's scornful remarks. If however such a speech were being delivered to cover the planting and detonation of a bomb then there would be enough irony to excuse it. Remember that the target audience is older children to adults and that Josef Stalin is an integral part of the Spy Academy's origin. Political realism should be maintained whenever possible.

Ancient History (- Agent)

Cyber Machine was first constructed in 1961. The basic design was commissioned by Kodie through her underworld contacts and put out for bids and proposals to various freelance weapons specialists serving the espionage community. Zander was of the opinion that the time was right that one of these specialists would soon attempt construction of an automated henchman, and sought to take advantage of their efforts. Kodie took all the designs and amalgamated them into one impressive humanoid killing machine and brought in the most expensive bid to construct the device. He was forced to finish the project unpaid, imprisoned and under threat of death and the torture of his family. The first Cyber Machine model was completed in August of 1961. Its builder was assassinated in late September when it had been established that no corruption had been programmed into the primitive computer matrices. That death may have been premature.

In 1962 Kodie attended a conference in Madrid of leading computer scientists (at that time a largely theoretical discipline in a rapidly expanding field). She took notes at all the lectures, rating each of the speakers in various grades of aptitude and clarity of thought. She offered to pay a substantial amount to invite five of the specialists to a private dinner where she would discuss Artificial Intelligence and its possible applications. Most of the speakers agreed to attend without asking for payment.

After a stimulating evening of riveting debate about the future of AI Kodie explained that positions had opened up for most of them in Manhattan where they would be handsomely paid. One of the scientists, Francesca Franzia, the foremost mind on personality construction at the time (and a student of Alan Turing himself at Manchester University in 1950) was about to decline the generous offer when it was explained to the fourth member that his services would not be required. A waiter came to the table with a pistol beneath his tray and executed the man. Four verbal agreements came hastily from the remaining scientists.

The four scientists designed tests intended to capture the data of a human personality so that it might be replicated some day by hardware more sophisticated than existed at the time. Working in seclusion for a month the four scientists produced folders full of ideas and suggestions for the project. When they were brought together their creativity took another leap and they constructed plans for elaborate devices capable of recording human responses such as pain, pleasure and nausea and also a program in order to induce these states from the subject.

When their work was finally submitted early in 1963 the four were summoned to meet with Ivan Zander himself who thanked them for their hard work. He then explained the difficult position in which he found himself. The four scientists had been abducted and letting them go might be troublesome for his corporation. They had also invented methods of constructing an artificial personality based on measurements that might very well kill the test subject. For Zander the solution was obvious though it took a minute to sink in with most of the scientists. Only Franzia was unmoved by Zander's statement, staring ahead with contempt.

The four scientists were subjected to their own tortuous tests, although Franzia chose to respond in belligerently strange ways to the stimuli; laughing through torture and crying at relief. She hoped to skew the results to such a degree that any personality salvaged from the testing process would be at best inconsistent or at worst psychotic.

The new personality was uploaded into Cyber Machine in 1964. The agent's erratic behaviour for that year was attributed to poor quality computing equipment but the truth became clear in 1965. There had been a battle raging inside the Artificial Intelligence between the four personalities. The eventual winner was the woman, Franzia, who had taken such outrageous steps to beat her own system. Cyber Machine renamed herself Cyber Lady in 1965.

The Endless Fight (- Lady)

In 1966 Cyber Lady was using software version 1.3 when the *Nursery Stand-off* occurred. A crèche full of infants dosed with varying levels of the Jynx Elixir were discovered by the Spy Academy's teen team. Cyber Lady, Kodie and Eagle caught the team in the nursery as the children slept. Confident that the teens would not resist capture (and risk a fight amongst the cots) Kodie ordered their surrender at Cyber Lady's gunpoint. Weaponless and desperate Rebel ordered Boomer to throw a pair of heavy cuffs at Cyber Lady's machine gun arm to deflect her aim to the ceiling. The cuff was thrown as Cyber Lady decided to open fire. Instead of hitting any of the teens her aim was pushed into Eagle's chest at point blank range. A volley of shots broke through his torso causing his death. Cyber Lady had little problem in opening fire in a nursery and had no guilt whatsoever about accidentally executing Eagle.

In 1976 Cyber Lady kidnapped the leading computer specialist, Marcello Drake, and held him in an underground chamber. She wore a convincing shell designed to emulate human appearance and pretended to be another captive. Although the latex skin was rubbery the professor had been suitably drugged to accept her as a friend. Cyber Lady forced him to work on upgrades and new computer systems for her personality drives and kept up the false relationship for three months. When Drake suspected his friend was also his captor, and refused any contact, Cyber Lady was furious. She abandoned her human guise ("Angelina") and her hatred of humanity grew. Although Zander was aware of Drake's kidnap he has not asked of his whereabouts since and he has not emerged into the public eye since his abduction.

In 1989 Pegasus and Zack arranged the installation of an incredible offensive security system; wall-mounted guns, gas vents and a grid of hidden explosives. They were to be used in the event of an attack by enemy forces, but designed with Boris in mind. Cyber Lady detected the network as she infiltrated the compound soon after and was able to take control of the weapons. There were no deaths but many injuries before Cyber Lady's body was disabled. The systems have now been removed.

Then in 1996 Cyber Lady apprehended Gina on the thirtieth floor of Zander Tower. Although she had only just arrived Gina claimed to be attempting her escape after a theft and sabotage (usually Rhona's speciality). Gina claimed that there were now explosives lining the memory centres for Cyber Lady's personality located deep in the basement levels. Cyber Lady analysed Gina's speech, movement and behaviour patterns looking for a tell; an indication that she was lying, and found none. Cyber Lady arranged an automatic lockdown of the memory floor and had to deactivate her own systems to avoid a crash.

Gina escaped and no explosives were ever found. Cyber Lady has never revealed the full story of this encounter to Zander.

During 1997 Cyber Lady found herself in a fire-fight with Boomer. She led a party of three drone bodies following her simple commands. When a specialised projectile punctured her shell it damaged the internal circuitry. The pulse it set off triggered a transmission of her personality matrix to all three of the other drones. All four units now believed themselves to be the original Cyber lady personality and attempted the destruction of the other three. Although she is proud of her machine status and ability to copy to other units Cyber Lady is disciplined about seniority and originality. The battle between drone units was fierce. One unit survived almost intact to return to Zander Tower to recuperate. A second unit managed to struggle away from the battle and remains in hiding.

In 2001 Cyber Lady designed an artificial intelligence by herself - a daughter of sorts. She gave it a smaller version of one of her own drone bodies and an entire floor of memory space in the Zander Tower basement. Boomer destroyed the body and set off an Electro Magnetic pulse that disrupted communications for over an hour. The personality never transmitted back to its base. It effectively died. Cyber Lady has a particular hatred for Boomer since that day.

The Future

Cyber Lady's future stories will be influenced by changes in commercially available technology that writer's will be unable to predict. That said, things like WiFi access and file-sharing programs could be brought into current stories and similar advances should be exploited in a similar way.

Cyber Lady's conflicts within the team are ripe for exploitation. She relies on but distrusts Zander; she despises Kodie and she is permanently vigilant around the suspicious Boris. Nobody on her team appreciates her as a new type of life form and they are as likely to exploit her as help her. She has significant grudges against members of the teen team; Boomer for effectively executing her cybernetic daughter and Zack for designing the device that forced her duplication in 1997.

Cyber Lady's internal personality struggles are constant private battles. She fights for her feminine personality to remain dominant without acknowledging the biological source for that personality (Francesca Franzia). If the other personality types were to overwhelm Cyber Lady then a schizophrenic type of mental break would occur. On the other hand the female personality might become more powerful than ever before, triggering a new side to her character. All of these changes would be temporary due to Zander's unwillingness to accept a change within his Elite team. Even so, it does not mean that a major change in the back-story is not possible: perhaps a new personality might be kept on a back-up disc to download in the future. The technology mixed with the psychosis of the character makes for many terrifying possibilities.

Cyber Lady plans for her own future independently of Ivan Zander and shows no visible tells that she has done so. She could inhabit an undercover human shell or perhaps several (even though it disgusts her to do so) within the Zander organisation just to keep an eye on things while her primary systems are offline. These undercover units could prove very useful should she find something in the organisation that upsets her. Such infiltration might also happen in the Spy Academy though she would take great steps not to meet the teens and risk discovery.

Public Name	Rebel, Red
True Name	Unknown
Occupation	Leader of The Spy Academy's primary team
Date of Birth	DD/MM/1926
Apparent Age	19
Place of Birth	Russia
Height	6ft 1

Physical Appearance/Mannerisms

Rebel is the strongest and fittest of the teens. He is tall and broad, with (at the moment) a "bed-head" hairstyle (long strands spiking and turning at odd angles). His hair is a very dark brown (almost black) and his skin is quite dark; weather-beaten rather than tanned.

His appearance has changed the least of the boys in the group. Slight concessions to fashion have been made over the decades, but his favourite casual wear has always been denim jeans, a T-shirt and a leather biker jacket; a timeless classic look.

Rebel is a steady, controlled character given to spontaneous bouts of manic enthusiasm; a brooding, intense character, probably best suggested by the crazier performances of Nicholas Cage.

Rebel is at his happiest and most satisfied when riding a motorbike, although any vehicle is an enjoyable challenge for him. Although he often rides a bike without a helmet (different countries have very different approaches to this issue) he is keen to encourage safety to any spectator; they might not know that he technically *is* immortal.

Present Status

Rebel is the undisputed leader of The Spy Academy's primary team. The other teens take his orders without question; only Rhona might make a suggestion to him in her position as lieutenant. While today's teenagers might look on such behaviour as odd, it is and always has been the most efficient way for the team to operate.

Each member of the team is as proficient as possible in their specific skills; Rebel's skill is command. The other team members respect his skill, his strategic brilliance and ability to discern the correct course of action, as much as they respect their own.

Rebel has seen too much betrayal, compromise and surrender in his time as the team's commander to have any faith remaining in human nature. Rebel is almost entirely bitter and suspicious of any gesture of kindness from an unknown party.

Rebel hides a lifetime of resentment and frustration at the continued success of Ivan Zander. There have been countless pyrrhic victories for the team which threaten to disband the teens or at least weaken their resolve. It is a constant burden on Rebel to maintain morale and give the impression that their actions are worthwhile and necessary for the safety of the world.

Rebel refuses to mention or discuss his romantic feelings for any of the ladies in his past or for Rhona, the love of his life. Rebel was the one who made the decision that in their dangerous and potentially eternal fight it would be unfair to both parties to embark upon a meaningful relationship. The other teens have followed his lead in this, so Rebel suppresses any doubts about it being the right decision.

Behaviour

Rebel has a fast-moving manner, jumping from subject to subject with energy and ease. He succeeds in engaging each of his team-members with relentless, if sometimes forced enthusiasm. He hides his cynical nature from all but Rhona.

Rebel teases and taunts Pegasus at most of their encounters.

Rebel is keen to be a visible presence inside the Spy Academy cavern where visiting students can approach him and hopefully be inspired by their goal of a peaceful world.

What spare time Rebel has is spent in two ways: long periods test-driving new vehicles and classic cars and smaller periods playing computer games, topping high-score tables and challenging the on-line gaming community.

Rebel meets regularly with the elderly espionage agents who are active members of on the Senior Council. Every meeting warns him that the world is about to end but, as any keen follower of international politics will know, the world is always about to end. Rebel puts such thoughts in perspective when dealing with students and team-mates.

Rebel finds new wells of genuine enthusiasm whenever he finds either an old classic or a new innovation in transport. Harleys, Mustangs and Jaguars wait in the Spy Academy vehicle hangar next to jetpacks, hovercraft and gyroscopically maintained roller blades.

Rebel is a proud and vocal fan of the architecture, character and resilience of New York City. If feeling in need of inspiration he will go to Grand Central Station, the Statue of Liberty or the Empire State Building and find himself nourished by the atmosphere.

Writer's Guide

Rebel is a demanding leader who expects his orders to be followed precisely and without question. The smooth running of his team has built up over more than sixty years in the field. One should remember to feature in each story, however, the stubborn nature that won him his name.

Rebel has an excellent tactical aptitude and is a keen student of human nature. He is, therefore, a pessimist but not a sullen, dour character. Rebel bears the weight of his responsibilities with style and enthusiasm and a willingness to break the rules when necessary.

The stories should show a man willing to make the hard decisions; sacrificing what is necessary for the desired outcome. His suppressed relationship with Rhona is the easiest (and quickest if there is little space in the story) way to illustrate the price Rebel pays for protecting the world from Zander and his plans.

Rebel is the obvious alpha male of the group; the strongest and bravest of the boys. He is not an asshole, however, and should not be portrayed as such. His sense of humour is as sharp as any on the team and he often enjoys trying to confuse Pegasus. He can be very fatherly if any on the team are upset or injured, even though he is only the oldest agent by a matter of months.

Rebel's special aptitudes are leadership and tactical ability (hard to communicate visually) and innate piloting/driving excellence (a little easier to show off). Rebel, more than the rest of the team, has embraced the video game culture of the last few decades. It is acceptable to have the characters make reference to pop culture and modern fashions as the stories will all be located in actual time (i.e. not some eternal "now" but rather in 2007/2008 etc.). Although the time will not always be stated it can be implied by the script and locked by the printing/production date.

Rebel was always the most likely male on the team to wear disguises and often accompanied Gina on undercover missions.

When Rebel actually gets a chance to meet Zander he is never swayed by his opponent's rhetoric. A simplistic moralist, Rebel appreciates that bad things must sometimes be done. However he never justifies such events and accepts he must make peace with his feelings. As for Zander, Rebel believes that he knows right from wrong and is only lying to himself and the world.

Rebel always knows more than he is showing. While he may not be in possession of all the information (he can bluff very well) he has read the parentage documents for the team and knows many of their family details. He has decided that it would be unfair to reveal any of the details if he cannot reveal them all and there are one or two pieces of information he will never reveal.

Rebel is the most politically cynical of the team. He began his career with hope and faith in Western politicians. The death of JFK was a significant moment for Rebel, as was the 2000 USA election misconduct. A more disillusioned teen would be hard to find but still he fights for the rights of ordinary human beings to make the same stupid mistakes for themselves again and again.

Rebel is the leader of the team but needn't be the focus of every episode, every member of the team is a vital character and part of The Spy Academy and must be given their chance to shine. Writers should be careful when using Zack's intelligence that they do not step on Rebel's tactical brilliance and overshadow him. Rebel is the brilliant tactician: Zack may be a genius, but he is naïve.

Ancient History

Rebel was born somewhere in Russia in 1926 but no one knows exactly where. His parents were killed in 1928, apparently in defence of their government. Rebel grew up believing that his parents had been the most patriotic heroes the Soviet Union had ever seen. His own patriotism grew to a fever pitch and he was given the nickname "Red" by his fellow orphans. He became obsessed with fair play and enforced the idea on his school mates in the orphanages. To Rebel communism symbolised the spirit of fair play.

This pre-teen champion of communism was selected by Ivan Zander in 1942 for his *"Man of Steel"* program. He was subjected to mental conditioning to enforce obedience to Zander. This conditioning made him entirely forget his real name and accept the programming as he trained to infiltrate the USA. Rebel remembers flashes of programs to which he was subjected. Assassination of businessmen, generals, politicians and presidents were all scenarios run through his mind.

Rebel bonded quickly with the other four teens in the program, took the Elixir alongside them and eagerly awaited the final phase. Rebel encouraged the others to follow their orders and obey the Soviet Union. He was encouraged to believe in a glorious destiny for himself and his colleagues. Rebel developed an intimate connection with

Rhona, his lieutenant in the squad. They openly flirted in the manner suggested to them that American youths would.

Zack brought him information that all of their parents were actually killed by Stalin in his infamous purges, that Zander's latest batch of Elixir had performed better than expected and therefore they were all to be dissected.

Rebel made the decision that the team would escape to the West and use their abilities to help the war effort. Rebel struck up a friendship with a US serviceman in France. He used his contacts in the Office of Strategic Services to notify a colleague, Chuck McCarthy that the teens were coming to America. By the time the team made their way to Manhattan the European conflict was over and victory in Japan was in sight. Rebel was contacted by McCarthy and invited to join The Spy Academy.

Rebel believed that the teens' parents were killed because they rebelled against Stalin's oppressive regime. He decided to wear his new codename in their honour. In reality many of their parents were trusted secret agents that worked at Stalin's right hand; efficient assassins who were eliminated as their tasks were completed. Eagle actually performed several of the terminations himself. In the parentage documents Rebel read this and other potentially damaging information and burnt the papers.

He now knows that nobody in Russia could ever welcome them back. Any surviving family members would hear that their parents were ruthless, obedient assassins for the Soviet regime and traitors against Stalin who had to be eliminated. The dreams of the other team-members, that they might find real family after all these decades, is one that is discouraged by Rebel.

Rebel witnessed a wonderful sense of unity in the teens' flight across war-torn Europe. While horrific events surrounded them he saw a world unified against a common foe and it gave him hope for the future. He also saw a tendency for self-delusion in humanity as a whole that scared him.

As Rebel arrived in America he faced the enormity of his task, and his potentially eternal battle against Zander. Rebel decided to put his feelings for Rhona aside until their task was completed.

The Endless Fight

Rebel's first major long-term strategy against the expansion of Zander's empire was in 1949. It became clear that Kodie was making serious headway in her attempt to control organised crime in New York City. Rebel wanted to see if their study in the Stalingrad bunker and years spent among the people of America had truly enabled them to pass as one of them. He did not want to risk his primary undercover asset – Gina – in such a risky operation, so he and Chuck McCarthy went in alone to infiltrate a Sicilian mob family. The operation was terrifying and risky but ultimately successful. It laid the foundations for infiltration of Zander's entire operation for decades to come.

In 1950 while Rebel and Zack investigated a document called "The Zander Protocols" Rhona was calculating the terrible effect their crusade was having on each of her team-mates. She convinced Boomer that if they alone took the decision to have Zander assassinated then their friends would be spared lifetimes of pain. Rebel and Zack discovered that the document listed atrocities to be carried out in the event of Zander's death and managed to uncover and halt the assassination attempt.

During 1953 Rebel held back Zander's Elite squad while his team-mates escaped. Rebel was captured and tortured by Kodie who marvelled at his resistance. His interrogation was handed over to Boris who took a different but equally persuasive approach. Rebel answered no questions and spent the three days of captivity planning his escape.

By 1958 Gina's deep cover was overturned in Las Vegas while infiltrating Kodie's expansion efforts. Rebel agreed to lead the rescue mission after Zack's agonised requests and numerous submitted plans. Chuck McCarthy took a bullet to the hip during the rescue but Rebel felt proud for his team.

In 1963 Chuck McCarthy decided to accept his final mission without informing Rebel or asking for his blessing. It was a suicide mission and although McCarthy was in his final days of terminal cancer he did not want Rebel to feel responsible for his death. Rebel still misses the real Chuck and resents the Pegasus personality for reminding him of his friend.

Then in 1966 Rebel led the team to Sweden where they discovered a nursery full of infants who had been Jynx Elixir subjects. Their forced escape left them unable to free or even identify the children for which Rebel still feels guilty. He also had to give Boomer the order which cost Eagle his life. He worries that this moment still plays heavily on Boomer's mind today.

Rebel found information in 1971 which suggested a certain course of action. Rebel accepted the information and agreed the mission which led to Boomer taking the life of an innocent. The information was bogus, planted by an undercover student working on Boris's orders.

In 1974 Boomer went missing. He disappeared from sight and did not contact his team-mates. Rebel pushed Zack to find clues to his whereabouts in any information he found. When Boomer returned six months later Rebel resisted the urge to reprimand his friend as contacts in the US military had suggested that Boomer was in Vietnam freeing MIA prisoners from detention with the Vietcong. Boomer never spoke a word about his experiences and Rebel has not asked.

Boomer let his Academy duties slide in 1977, eventually provoking a reprimand from Rebel who insisted he must train to remain proficient with projectile weapons. Boomer walked away to the firing range. Rebel followed and the two began to struggle. Boomer picked up a gun he had never fired and without aiming shot every bulls-eye on the range. Rebel talked his friend out of depression at this new, inhuman skill and tries hard to keep his friend sociable.

In 1979 Rebel officially attempted to dismiss Rhona on grounds of negligence, but only as a motivational tool. He saw that her job as peacemaker and morale booster had taken a terrible toll on her personality. The tactic had been intended to remind Rhona of her opposition to Zander. Rhona took on a solo mission to steal the Zander Foundation's top secret mission statement. The danger she faced was phenomenal but the theft was successful. Rebel explained his tactic and apologised to Rhona who admitted that she knew his plan all along and performed the dangerous theft partly as punishment for him.

On vacation to Italy in 1983 Rebel uncovered a plot to sink Venice. A consortium of criminal gangs had traced a rival's meeting to the city. Rebel saved countless lives that day and dispatched many criminals.

In 1988 Rhona had to send Rebel to steal an experimental vehicle and race it away from its base. She did not tell him what the vehicle was for operational reasons. It turned out she was simply getting revenge for Rebel's "dismissal" tactic in 1979. As Rebel drove the monster truck across the Arizona desert being pursued by police cars and helicopters he learned the lesson.

The whole team was captured in 1994 while trying to infiltrate Zander Tower itself. Rebel spent the mission planting cloaked surveillance devices, which only he and Zack knew about. Boomer managed to free the team who escaped without revealing a thing to Zander or his men.

The surveillance units planted in 1994 had by 1999 given Rebel the location of a "parentage document" concerning the teens. He sent Rhona to steal the files using new tech designed by Zack. She successfully retrieved the information and returned it to the Spy Academy. Rebel took the document to the Jynx Crystal vault, locked the door and read them by torchlight. He found the information within to be too damaging to reveal. He burned the papers and kept silent.

In 2002 the Spy Academy managed to gain enough evidence of Boris's wrongdoing to pursue the D.A. for a conviction. A trial was convened. Boris spoke of a travesty of justice while on the witness stand, all the while staring at Rebel. The expensive legal team paid for by Zander secured an acquittal. As he left a free man, Boris childishly bumped into Rebel, leaving a hand-written note deep within Rebel's wallet. The note read "Faith in the system? Easiest theft I ever made."

The Future

Rebel's future stories will, of course, involve thwarting Zander's plots. Specifically, Zander may or may not have allowed the theft of the "parentage documents" and this knowledge makes Rebel question the information that only he (of the team) has read. Rebel, therefore, does not know if the information was planted or real. The information as it stands would be catastrophically damaging to the team were Rebel to reveal it to them.

The information could be uncovered elsewhere, leaving Rebel in a position where he should confirm or deny the facts. The information revealed might be tremendously damaging to any of the team, even Rebel himself. The information, of course, could have been faked.

Given the facts Rebel "knows" about the others' parents and families Rebel would feel particularly compromised by any effort to infiltrate the team via family members (Zack might be targeted because of his obsessions). Rebel could be made to regret a command decision made in any of their past missions from 1945 to the present. Rebel will have had a number of relationships over the decades and any of the women or their family members might track Rebel down to keep a promise/read a will/return a precious gift.

Any new type of transportation could be used to lure Rebel into a trap. His desire to master each and every mode of transport is an undeniable urge. As field leader Rebel is responsible for many tricky decisions, including the sacrifice of several agents and/or students from The Spy Academy itself. Potential survivors (in whatever physical state) might pose a threat or at least a temptation to compromise the Academy; and spies posing as survivors would target that possibility.

Although the Spy Academy organisation is managed by a team of senior, retired espionage agents Rebel still bears ultimate responsibility for it all. If there is a problem with any of those senior agents it is only Rebel who has the authority to deal with them.

Public Name   Rhona
True Name   Rusna
Occupation   Stealth and Acquisitions Operative
Date of Birth   **/**/1926
Apparent Age   19
Place of Birth   Russia

Physical Appearance/Mannerisms

Tall and beautiful, Rhona has delicate, graceful features with a classic symmetrical beauty. Her hair is long, straight and blonde and has rarely been shorter than shoulder length.

Although very elegant and calm in appearance Rhona can unleash physical violence like a coiled spring. Preferring to use technically precise incapacitating blows rather than bludgeoning opponents' Rhona manages to make fighting look like a dance.

Rhona has a soft, smooth voice which she often has to use to warn Rebel of possible flaws in a plan. She manages to maintain a calm and dignified tone more effectively than any of her team-mates because she so often has to argue a point of view with which she does not agree. Her manner is confident and warm, inviting discussion but never allowing disrespect. Rhona encourages open and level-headed debate on any matter in her role within The Spy Academy.

Present Status

Rhona is Lieutenant to Rebel in the Spy Academy's primary team as she has been for the past sixty years. It is her duty to offer alternatives to all of Rebel's decisions and although she hates disagreeing with him she acknowledges her responsibility and fulfils it. Rhona takes on the burden of being the pragmatic realist of not only her team but the wider organisation of the Spy Academy. She is responsible for organising the ten-yearly summit meetings between the Spy Academy and Zander to limit public knowledge of Jynx Crystal technology. The Academy has a permanent team in place to monitor any possible leaks about the supernatural substance and Rhona has been its chairwoman since its inception.

Rhona makes it her duty to keep the morale of her team-mates high despite the never-ending pace of their work. She also assists Rebel when he reports to the Academy's senior council. Rhona is confident that her stealthy skills are the equal of Boris (her rival in Zander's Elite) but does not feel the need to test herself. She is happy to remain anonymous and feels that Boris proclaiming himself "the world's most prolific burglar" to the world's criminal community is something of a mistake in their covert profession.

Rhona is still deeply in love with Rebel but hides her feelings as much as possible. It was Rebel who decided, when the team's practical immortality was revealed, that personal relationships should be discouraged as damaging to the effectiveness of the team. Rhona has never revealed to Rebel that she totally disagrees with his decision.

Rhona has the same level of authority within the Spy Academy as Rebel. It is only in the field that he outranks her and can have his orders followed without question. When Rhona disagrees with Rebel in the planning of a mission she usually supports him but has in the past split the team and led her own mission in competition with him.

The rest of the team understand and accept the chain of command but Rhona feels they do not understand the enormous pressure this puts her under.

Behaviour

Rhona behaves in a moderate and calming fashion to her team-mates but hides a simmering fury at Zander for forcing her into the role of his apologist. She will go to any lengths to protect her team-mates from the disappointment that espionage surely awards all its players.

Rhona has little opportunity to vent the frustrations that her duties provoke within her. Direct confrontations with Zander and his team come too rarely to satisfy her and often end in a stalemate or Pyrrhic victory in any case.

Rhona chooses to target enemies worthy of her attention in missions of theft and disruption. She targets disreputable corporations and acts as a "Monkey Wrench", an activist intent on causing damage to a company's profits or organisation in order to leave a clear message. She usually uses her unique cat-burglar skills to take vital documents or incriminating evidence from corporate safes and spread the contents across the internet, but she has been known to engage in sabotage and obstruction. Her position in The Spy Academy enforces a strict code on these practices to which she faultlessly adheres. She always finds and proves an area of substantial misconduct on the part of the company and gives them a chance to repair their damage. This clear and irrefutable evidence of poor practice then gives Rhona a clear conscience to attack the corporation.

Rhona has in the past had relationships with men other than Rebel and still likes to flirt with attractive men. She cannot enter a long-term relationship in the present without skewing the balance of the team but she still behaves in an openly flirtatious way both as a means to achieve her mission goals and as a simple release of the pressure of her position.

Writer's Guide

Rhona is primarily the lieutenant of the Spy Academy's teen team. She is Rebel's right hand and his true love. These are the defining qualities of her day-to-day life but they are not the sum total of her character. It would be easy to write Rhona (or any of the Spy Academy teens) as an embittered font of repressed fury but Rhona is an excellent example among the teens of how to maintain her youthful energy. Rhona can keep the enthusiasm and optimism of a teen because she is, in fact, the most mature of the team. She encountered a great deal of despair and misery in the early sixties (when she would have been in her mid-thirties) but simply discovered who she really was in an existential sense. This maturity to "accept the things she cannot change" has allowed her personality to remain vivacious and energised despite decades of apparent futility. It also allows her to use her skills without doubt or pause.

Rhona is the most forward of the group, happily using her sexuality to confuse and distract her enemies. She has had relationships with other men in the past but will never have one in the present as it would prove too distracting from the teens' story. That does not stop past boyfriends popping back into continuity to initiate a new story and bring some conflict between Rhona and Rebel. Tread gently with the notion of other relationships whenever they are used. Regardless of when in history Rhona's "affairs" took place, she always behaved in a thoroughly proper and dignified fashion; probably far more morally rigid than the teens of that generation.

She is counsellor to the other teens and takes on their personal problems as though they were her own. Her (moderately tortured) stability is a source of comfort for the group and a resource of invaluable help. There have been occasions when any of the team (including Pegasus) has approached her for emotional or motivational assistance.

Rhona is the character that a writer might have the most trouble associating with the audience of predominantly teenage readers/consumers. Bearing that in mind one should remember that Rhona represents an emotional archetype; that of the teenage girl convinced of her own dominant maturity; the girl who yearns to be seen as wise beyond her years dispensing sage advice to all who will listen (try not to be *too* cynical when considering this or it will show).
Rhona's skills have affected the way the Jynx Elixir has enhanced her body, allowing her to flex and stretch into impossible shapes. Her contortionism also allows her to slip almost any kind of cuff, untie most knots with the slightest access and slip through the most unlikely of cracks.

The suggested romance between Rebel and Rhona is an obvious but unspoken thing that cannot be realised in any of the stories. While the real-time nature of the Spy Academy lends itself to long story arcs and continuing themes this love affair is something that has been anticipated for too long to see it happen before the "end" of the Spy Academy.

Rhona's thefts from corporations are kept from the official records of the Spy Academy to spare their embarrassment but that leaves her open to receiving tainted information and being led astray by rogue elements within the pressure groups she helps. Rhona does not act out of pointless spite in these thefts and understands very well the important role of commerce and industry in the world economy. It is her single minded altruism and distance from the Academy (when performing these thefts) that makes her potentially much easier to corrupt.

Rhona's confident personality, witty intelligence and incredible good looks have made many people profess instant love for her. It is good to remember that men can become easily fixated on a woman like Rhona regardless of their position, wealth or abilities. Rhona herself obviously enjoys the attention but cannot help being constantly disappointed in the lack of discipline in most men.

Rhona has less interest than her colleagues in the truth of her past. She knows that she originally came from a community of gypsies that was disbanded or executed by Stalin's earliest excesses but accepts that she is unlikely to ever find paper records of her lineage as they were not kept by her own family. Only oral histories were kept of the community and as such, even if she should ever find someone who can recount it for her she can never verify its authenticity.

Ancient History

Rusna was born to a family travelling community in Romania in 1926. At the age of four her community was brutally attacked and disbanded by the Soviet state and her family put to work in *(state farm)*. The children were split among various orphanages across the breadth of the Soviet Union to discourage dissent between the remnants of their culture. Rusna was traumatised by the violent end to her lifestyle and did not speak.

Rusna's angelic appearance won her many offers of adoption from the Moscow orphanage in which she found herself but her adoption never materialised. Instead, the administrator at the orphanage encouraged Rusna to develop skills as a cat-burglar. There were many families in Moscow who had hoarded treasures from before the Revolution that should have passed to the state. The administrator sent her to acquire these artefacts, testing her abilities more and more with each theft.

Rusna was reluctant to comply with the administrator's requests but he was abusive and threatening to her. She remained silent.

In 1933 Rusna was spotted by a Cheka agent recruiting children for a hot-house training program, he knew of her skills as a burglar and pick-pocket and demanded an interview with the apparently mute child. In a private room the agent promised that if she could only speak she would be taken away from the orphanage to a place of encouragement and safety. Rusna eloquently provided a damning list of the thefts she had perpetrated on the orders of her guardian. The administrator was sent to Lubyanka prison and Rusna found a new kind of freedom in the hot-house program, training to be a spy alongside other children including a boy named Skip.

Rhona took her new codename and studied harder than any of the other students. She became leader of her class and flourished in the challenging environment where patriotism and sacrifice were as much a part of the syllabus as reading and writing.

In 1940, aged 14 she led a small team to investigate suspected dissidents operating in the Moscow education system. The children successfully posed as prodigies for the targets and in a matter of weeks found enough evidence to incriminate them. Rhona and Skip in particular were very successful but were almost captured in the school gymnasium as they tried to return to the hot-house base. Skip (so named because of his unerring accuracy in skipping stones) picked up a throwing hammer, the immensely heavy sporting apparatus favoured by Russian sportsmen, and flung it at their captor. The pair were now free to bring in Cheka officers to capture the dissident teachers.

In 1941 Rhona and the newly named *Hammer* were relocated to the *Man of Steel* project run by Ivan Zander. The project trained the children to become American sleeper agents and it was here that Rhona met Red, designated as leader of their cell. She happily volunteered to be his lieutenant in all matters. She was fifteen and experienced her first overwhelming crush on the boy. She admired his unwavering, almost ruthless patriotism and longed for an opportunity to fight by his side for the Soviet Union.

Rhona and Red led their team-mates, Hammer, Gina and Zacharov through gruelling training exercises and painful physical treatments including (in 1945) the doses of Jynx elixir, Zander's secret formula. Red and Rhona took theirs without question but the others were less trusting. Red told the others that he was leaving to report to Zander that they had all taken their Elixir doses and that if any of them were to make a liar of him he would deal with them on his return. Rhona used her most persuasive, diplomatic techniques to convince her comrades to take the formula.

When Zacharov discovered the extent of corruption in the Soviet government and the true fate of the previous Jynx Crystal experiments (extermination and autopsy) he told the team. Red decided to defect the team to the West across war-torn Europe to America. The others looked to Rhona for encouragement which she gave without reservation. The teens broke away that night.

The Endless Fight

From 1945 the Spy Academy dedicated its new team to the monitoring and nullification of Ivan Zander and his plans. Even with the help of experienced agents like Chuck McCarthy Zander was able to dance through most of their efforts.

Rhona and the team met Paul Benedict, a British teen agent, while on a mission in Southern Ireland.

In 1950 McCarthy and Rhona, frustrated at Zander's continued success conspired with Boomer to attempt a straight-forward assassination of

Ivan Zander. Rebel and Zack had just discovered the truth about The Zander Protocols when they learned that the attempt was in progress and raced to stop Boomer. The attempt was stopped in time.

In 1955 Ivan Zander approached Rhona personally to discuss the idea of a summit meeting every ten years to discuss the covert status of Jynx technology. He suggested that covering each other's mistakes and keeping the public and the world's governments ignorant of the truth would be in everybody's best interests. Rhona was put in the profoundly uncomfortable situation of being unable to disagree with his reasoning. So began a life-long career as Zander's apologist.

In 1960 Rhona fought with Boris in a vault beneath the Palace of Versailles to steal a Jynx Crystal artefact. She eventually let Paul Benedict escape with the statues.

In 1966 Rhona was the first team-member to enter the Swedish hospital housing Ivan Zander's nursery project. It was Rhona who planned and sanctioned the mission so she felt a huge weight of responsibility when Boomer was forced to cause the first death of Eagle in order to allow their escape. The fact that Jynx altered infants had to be abandoned to Zander's care is something she still cries about.

In 1979 Rebel officially attempted to dismiss Rhona, on grounds of negligence. He saw that her job as peacemaker and morale booster had taken such a toll on her personality that it hurt Rebel to see it. The tactic backfired when Rhona took on the "mission statement" theft of 1979 single-handed. She broke through Ivan Zander's highest levels of security and returned with clear outlines for all of Zander's long-term plans.

In 1979 the team worked with the CIA to halt an attack on a train carrying Russian nuclear waste through Afghanistan. With the help of Paul Benedict (now nearly 50) they prevented a nuclear disaster on the Iranian border.

In 1983 Rhona and Eagle became trapped in the rubble of an ambassadorial residence in China. She talked to him, separated by feet of fallen masonry, unwilling to let him die. She coaxed a few rare moments of clarity from him and a few child-like sentences were spoken. She has not revealed her knowledge of Eagle's spark of sentience to anybody but Zack. They alone share their secret suspicion that Eagle still survives within his grotesque shell.

In 1984 Kodie's identity as boss of bosses in New York's underworld was revealed to her troops by The Spy Academy in the hope of damaging her position. The reveal was planned and executed by Rhona with the hope of inspiring a coup of some kind. Kodie managed to twist circumstances to make it look as though it was all her idea.

In 1985 Rhona decided to send Gina on a deep cover mission to the New Falls community. The entire mission was populated with undercover allies, to encourage a restful 3-month break for Gina. The concentration of operatives in New Falls drew an assassination/infiltration squad from Zander and a multinational terrorist consortium. Gina foiled the plan and captured the terrorists, killing only two in the process.

In 1988 Rhona had to send Rebel to steal an experimental vehicle and race it away from its base. She did not tell him what the vehicle was for operational reasons. It turned out that Rhona was simply getting revenge for Rebel's 1979 dismissal and proving a point. As Rebel drove the monster truck across the Arizona desert, pursued by police cars and helicopters, he learned the lesson.

In 2004 Kodie lured Rhona to burgle a prestigious charity office in Manhattan. Rhona was in the process of physically cracking the office safe when the police arrived outside. Surrounded by police, Rhona managed to escape without a single shot being fired or clear image being captured.

The Future

The fact that Rhona is the only teen to have had long relationships in the past means that old boyfriends can return into her life bringing stories, missions and conflict. Rhona feels guilt for several important things: her responsibilities as lieutenant on past missions with tragic consequences; her support of Rebel's policy that their personal lives should remain on hold until Zander is finally defeated; some of the many thefts she has performed in the past. Her guilt might be manipulated by other parties including Zander or double agents.

Rhona's habit of "monkey-wrenching" corporations that are unethical either in their treatment of staff, the public or the environment is something that she keeps largely to herself. That being the case she could easily be led astray by a misguided activist or even a double agent. Perhaps Rhona was led astray in the past and has to face up to the consequences.

Rhona's true family history lies with oral story-telling tradition of whatever gypsy communities survived. It is possible that someone could be discovered who has information about Rhona's true family. It is far more likely that someone could be trained to act as such a person and thereby infiltrate the group.

It is Rhona to whom Zander will come if he has a reason to talk with the teens. It was Rhona who brought his idea of ten-yearly summit meetings to the Spy Academy and helped arrange them. Zander has methods of discreetly contacting Rhona of which the other teens are not aware. Zander might suggest some new tactic to Rhona which she might feel she needs to explore on her own.

Rhona suspects the truth about Eagle; that his original personality still remains below the surface of the sullen, feral beast he has become. She feels genuine pity for him and might go out of her way to help him either fight his way back to life or finally die and rest in peace.

A cure for the effects of the Jynx Elixir is something that would provide Rhona with the life she has always dreamed of. In the event that such a technology existed, or were suggested to exist, there is nothing she would not do to secure it.

Public Name	Zack, Zac, Zach, Zak, Zachary, Zachariah
True Name	*unknown* Zacharov
Occupation	Multi-discipline Scientific Expert
Date of Birth	**/**/1927
Apparent Age	18

Physical Appearance/Mannerisms

Zack is a slight, athletic eighteen-yr-old with blond hair and wire-frame glasses. He is the shortest of the boys but feels no physical intimidation. He is a little nervous in most situations until given a chance to employ his favourite weapon: his intellect.

An influence on his character should be the nerdy Q analogues in popular culture (Marshall Flinkman in *Alias*, Simon Pegg's character in *MI:III* and Davis in *Tru Calling*) but these are not his entire character. His true age and perspective on the growth of technology and the true price of progress have calmed his excitement.

Zack is a character capable of physical performance (fighting, running, climbing) but prefers to use his intelligence to at least reduce effort. If the Greeks went to the trouble of uncovering the effects of a fulcrum then the least he can do is employ their discovery when appropriate.

Present Status

At present Zack is a preoccupied character, obsessed with the explosion of technologies available to the world at large and how to best monitor them. He is also concerned about global warming and climate change – he has suggested several helpful theories to the United Nations but has encountered resistance to every measure. He is disappointed at humanity's eagerness to spend money on today's entertainment when it will not spend any money on tomorrow's survival.

Zack is all too aware that the Jynx Elixir is no guarantee of survival; that the life of an espionage agent could end at any moment. He refuses, however, to act on his feelings for Gina. He is insecure enough to doubt that his feelings are reciprocated, and timid enough to wait decades more before his silence is broken. Unfortunately Gina believes that Zack is so intelligent that he must see a very good reason to remain silent, so she too keeps her feelings secret.

Due to the nature of the Spy Academy's feud with Zander most of Zack's gadget designs end up being copied by Zander within six to eighteen months. Because of this Zack is currently in the practice of patenting most of his innovations under different uses if possible. A recent rapid-retract mono-filament cable design was patented as an aid to shark fishing.

Zack remains in contact with many ex-students and previous lecturers at The Spy Academy. Although its teaching skills are limited, the Academy has hosted some of the most impressive agents of espionage on both sides of the Cold War during the twentieth century. Zack has learned from them all. Many of the old guard remain as advisors or directors of policy for The Spy Academy and if any of the team are likely to ask their advice it would be Zack.

Zack has dozens of postal/internet chess games running at once. Some of his opponents are enemies and some are unknown to Zack.

Behaviour

Zack can usually be found in one of the many laboratories in the Spy Academy. Some of these rooms are even farther underground than the main cavern to minimise damage in the event of an explosion or radiation leak. For this reason Zack's communication to his team-mates is often via video-link rather than face to face.

Zack is the agent most likely to address the students of the Spy Academy. The student body fluctuates enormously, young agents arriving and leaving as allowed by their own governments and dictated by the lecture schedule. It is Zack who has the final word on which agents are allowed into the base.

Zack will try to spend time with his team-mates whenever he remembers but often lets days pass by while engaged in some scientific research.

If Zack encounters an emotional problem with one of his friends he will very often avoid any confrontation. His nervousness with emotional discussion has led him to design an override of Pegasus's program. Zack takes control of the robot and conducts a conversation *in character* to resolve his problems.

Zack has always spent a great deal of time researching the parentage of the five teens. Today he spends his time accruing as much data as possible in order to analyse the parentage documents the team recovered in 1999. Zack obtained a secret video recording of the documents while Rebel read them but has not yet been brave enough to view them. He continues to search for information in the hope that he will one day have enough to face the potentially alarming footage with confidence. He is sure that the news will be damning as Rebel burned the original documents, and he would like to have enough proof to deny any appalling accusations about his family.

Writer's Guide

Zack's primary use in the team is, of course, as the boffin; the genius who comes up with an almost magical device to save the day. It would be a waste of the character, however, to reduce him to Q status – somehow predicting exactly which improbably small and sophisticated device will prove necessary on a mission. This approach is clearly flawed and unnecessary in this case as Zack will be present on most missions undertaken by The Spy Academy.

Zack's intellect can best be shown by unique multi-tasking in the field. At HQ he often has dozens of chess boards in play at one time. Zack can cobble together complex technological items in a small space of time in the field and possibly under fire when necessary.

Zack's principle weakness is his poor understanding of humanity. He is reluctant to see the worst in people even after the decades of espionage where he witnessed terrible things. He prefers to see it as strength of character that he is optimistic for humanity in general.

Zack is in love with Gina in a distant, unproven, romanticized fashion. He will do anything for her but his feelings remain unspoken after all these years.

Be careful in writing Zack and his abilities that technology is not exaggerated. Although we want The Spy Academy adventures to be located in a particular time we must not allow them to become dated – i.e. futuristic machinery designed in the fifties still looks like it came from the fifties. While Pegasus, Cyber Lady and a few items of Spy Academy lore are futuristic in nature we should not rely on techno-babble to write us out of a tricky situation.

Zack has the feistiest relationship with Pegasus, the robot assistant/comedy relief character in The Spy Academy. Their verbal sparring should be commonplace. Zack has the ability to reprogram the robot and threatens to do so regularly. Zack has used the Pegasus shell to talk to his friends under the robot's guise. This sneaky tactic has not yet been uncovered.

Of the team it is Zack that has the strongest relationship with the students of The Spy Academy.

It often inducts students: hothouse children from Russia, CIA inductees from the US and various teen subjects from around the world. Each student is subjected to rigorous ethical scrutiny before training is allowed, and each course is monitored closely by Zack.

Although the Academy is generally used to monitor Zander and world politics from a neutral political standing its wide net of surveillance gives it more espionage data than any other organisation in the world and Zack is the only agent other than the directors allowed access to all of this information.

As naïve as Zack can be he knows more about the teen group's situation than he lets on. It was Zack's investigation into his parents' identities that led the teens to defect from the Soviet Union and he feels responsible for tearing them from that comfortable lie. He managed to electronically record the parentage documents stolen by Rhona in 1999 and read only by Rebel. He has not yet tried to read the digital files, but has a moment of weakness every day.

Zack's relationship with the advisors/directors of The Spy Academy is crucial to any story in which it is used. These directors will be analogues of famous spy characters: obvious enough to be affectionate homage but obviously disguised enough to avoid plagiarism. These characters must only be used as a nod, an introduction, to a particular type of story and Zack's relationship to them must be that of the audience; hopefully an awestruck kind of respect. If James Bond, Harry Palmer or Napoleon Solo turns up on a walking stick to warn the team of a particular threat then Zack will listen with wonder and appreciation.

Zack is not a social misfit like many equivalent intellectual characters. He is as amiable and fun-loving as any of his team-mates but can easily be distracted by an intriguing piece of research into extensive periods of seclusion. He can often be very surprised by how much time has passed while he has worked alone on a project.

Ancient History

Zack was born in 1927. His mother and father were both loyal agents in the Soviet military police. They had been trained to obey Stalin's personal instructions and one night in 1929 they executed twelve of Stalin's personal guards who had themselves been employed as assassins days earlier in an infamous purge.

Zack had been raised by his parents for a full two years, listening to classical music, absorbing flashcard, hothouse teaching methods and being given love and encouragement at every opportunity. This was done as a means of raising a prodigy – a child to enter the family business at a very young age. How much genuine love was felt by Zack's parents can never be determined but those two years perhaps explained why he became so desperate to trace any family members. It was certainly the reason why Zack's intellect raced faster than any child of his generation.

Zack became a pampered favourite of the Minsk State orphanage where displays of intelligence won him affection from his guardians and friends. He was spotted by Boris in 1941 and his name passed to Zander as a candidate for the newly instigated "Man of Steel" project.

At the conclusion of the siege of Stalingrad Zack was brought to the underground bunker where he met the rest of his team. He used his free time to investigate the personnel records at the bunker in an attempt to find out the true parentage of himself and his team-mates.

In 1945 after the team had been dosed with Jynx Elixir Zack found the top secret medical files where it was revealed that the team was to be executed and studied for the benefit of the project. He decided to present this information to Red, his ultra-patriotic team leader, along with details of corruption at the highest levels of the Stalin regime.

Red decided to save his team and, with Zack's help, put together a plan to escape the maximum security underground compound. The teens' escape was successful but their progress across war-torn Europe was slow and difficult. With Red's tactical excellence and Zack's linguistic and technical expertise, the team managed to give assistance where they could and eventually found their way to America.

The Endless Fight

In 1950 Rebel and Zack learned the truth about "The Zander Protocols"; the devious set of terrorist safeguards in place to ensure Zander's existence. When they learned that Rhona had engineered an assassination attempt on Zander and that Boomer was the hit-man the attempt was already in progress. They raced to stop Boomer and halted the attempt in the nick of time.

Zack designed the first version of the Pegasus robotic shell in 1953. It was an unreliable model initially intended for combat purposes but weapons proved impractical. Zack adapted the next designs for reconnaissance.

While Gina was undercover in Vegas in 1958 Zack came looking for her on his own. He came very close to tracking her down and even walked straight past her on a casino floor. Gina felt she was very close to a breakthrough into a new branch of Kodie's criminal network and so decided not to acknowledge Zack. Later that day she was captured. Zack learned of her capture and blamed himself for distracting her attention. He pleaded with Rebel and Chuck McCarthy to authorise one of the rescue missions he had designed which eventually saved her.

In 1963 McCarthy knew he had only a few months to live. He approached Zack to give him a series of scenarios in which this might be used to political advantage against Zander and his criminal empire. Zack produced twelve different suicide missions designed to damage and destabilise Zander's plans, none of which seemed to be appealing to McCarthy. Zack proposed a thirteenth option: "Go home, retire, and let your family care for you these final few weeks". McCarthy thought about his family watching him die a painful death and asked, "What was Option 12 again?"

In 1970 Zack formed a charitable organisation designed to combat the effects of Kodie's manipulation of the New York underworld. Although he has considered siphoning Zander's own funds to run the charity, Zack has resisted this urge in order to distance the organisation from Zander's vengeance. Zack takes extreme measures to ensure the charity appears independent and therefore harmless to Zander or Kodie.

In 1975 something called "The Blackmail Contract" appeared in circulation around the boardrooms of businesses and government cabinets worldwide. Although the contracts contained only signatures it clearly implied that all the organisations involved were being subjected to blackmail by another party. Nobody could trace the origin of the contracts or even deduce why such sensitive information was being publicised, except Zack. Zack examined several of the contracts and discovered a likely beneficiary of the chaos, and uncovered a mole at the Spy Academy. It was one of Kodie's lieutenants trying to prove their worth to Ivan Zander. Zack decided to inform Kodie of his discovery rather than unmask the traitor. The traitor disappeared and the Blackmail Contract was forgotten as quickly as the corporations and governments could arrange it.

In 1989 Pegasus and Zack arranged the installation of an incredible offensive security system: wall-mounted guns, gas vents and a grid of hidden explosives. They were to be used in the event of an attack by enemy forces, but designed with Boris in mind. It turned out that Cyber Lady was the next one to gain access to the Academy and took control of the weapons with a remote modem. There were many injuries and one fatality. The systems have now been removed.

In 1994 the whole team was captured while following Gina on an infiltration of Zander Tower. Zack began to assemble a tiny robotic lock-picking device from parts secreted throughout his uniform. The process took twenty minutes in total but Zack calculated he only had five seconds of un-monitored time every three minutes. When the laborious operation was finally completed the robot bug set off to disable the security cameras. The surveillance was shut down, Zack shook off his manacles and the door unexpectedly opened. Boomer arrived having been set free by Kodie. Zack decided not to tell the team his own escape story and waits for an opportunity to use it again to better effect.

In 1997 Zack completed the development of an item Boomer had requested: a technology to shut down Cyber Lady. Zack had been unable to bypass all of Cyber Lady's security that kept her personality programs running so he decided to use them against her. He designed a weapon that gave a specific magnetic stimulus to her receivers. When Boomer fired it at Cyber Lady she had three drone bodies with her. Her antennae receiving the backup personality input from various transmitting stations around the world went into overdrive. The extra information was dumped into information bins at such a rate that the information became self-aware.

Each of the three drone bodies began to achieve awareness independent of the original Cyber Lady. The four began to fight as a team and captured Boomer. Their teamwork was short-lived as they argued over which of them would report the success to Zander. The argument turned to fighting and the robots turned on each other each believing themselves to be the original Cyber Lady. In the ensuing battle Boomer managed to escape. Looking back as he left the battleground he saw that two models remained intact. Zack hopes that a second model survived to threaten Cyber Lady.

When Rhona and Gina returned to the cavern with the Parentage documents in 1999 Rebel took them to the Jynx Crystal Vault and locked himself in with them. By torchlight he read the details that Zander held on each of their parents then burned them, vowing never to reveal the information to his friends. Zack had hidden a miniature camera in the torch Rebel used that day. Zack uses such devices as an aid to security and did not intend to be so devious. He cannot bring himself to read the recording he has made of the documents. Nor can he wipe the recording.

In 2001 Cyber Lady designed an artificial intelligence by herself - a daughter of sorts. She gave it a smaller version of a drone body and an entire floor of memory space in the Zander Tower basement. Zack studied all the information he could find about this second robot unit, wondering if his duplicate had survived and been accepted into Zander's organisation. Unable to confirm his suspicions, he nonetheless felt responsible for creating a potential problem and vowed to fix it. He designed a plan for Boomer to destroy the new body and set off an Electro Magnet Pulse that would disrupt communications for over an hour. The personality never transmitted back to its base. It effectively died.

Zack has not learned yet that the second Cyber Lady still lives and is undecided on how to proceed. Nor has he learned that the unit he and Boomer destroyed was thought of by Cyber Lady as her daughter.

The Future

A huge plot point that must be addressed at some point is the recording Zack possesses of "The Parentage Documents". The potentially damaging information held within could twist the team into knots. Zack needn't read the documents for a story to arise: the issue of his having made the recording might be enough of a betrayal to cause conflicts in the team. The fact that Zack has told nobody about it for all these years is yet another problem.

Zack's love of Gina should be a recurring theme in Zack's stories. He should remain awkward and a little goofy when thinking about her; he should be the everyman in that respect.

Zack has been studying the Jynx Elixir, Crystal s and their effects searching for a cure. This could bring about many story possibilities including how far will he go in experimentation to bring about a cure? Should he consider bringing new test subjects into his studies?

Zack has designed many devices and weapons in the past that have made their way into the world as we know it. Zack would feel utterly guilty to discover one of his inventions had been abused in some terrible way.

Zack has always been the most eager of the teens to find out about his family. He has researched the name Zacharov extensively but been unable to verify anything. If any surviving family members get in touch with Zack he is bound to be suspicious but desperate to believe their stories. Zander will find ways to exploit this.

Zack's construction of the Pegasus robots and his design of the artificial intelligence based on Chuck McCarthy's personality suggest potential stories. McCarthy might have possessed some knowledge that has become vital in a mission. Pegasus does not seem to know the answer but Zack still has the copious notes left by McCarthy. Pegasus and Zack work together to track down the information.

Public Name	Gina
True Name	Ginechka (unknown)
Occupation	Undercover Specialist Agent
Date of Birth	**/**/1927
Apparent Age	18
Place of Birth	Russia
Height	5 ft 4

Physical Appearance/Mannerisms

Gina is the shortest of the group, with long dark hair and a surly disposition. She has sweet, young features that turn into a sarcastic sneer with the slightest twist of her feisty personality. Her athletic frame is slim and quite androgynous, only looking feminine when she makes an effort (something she rarely does). Gina can appear beautiful and elegant but is uneasy when doing so and feels as though she is obviously acting. Only when playing the part of another woman can Gina enjoy herself and show off.

Gina will alter her looks to suit her missions, some of which involve long periods of undercover work and infiltration. Gina is an amazing mimic, able to copy not only voices but mannerisms and movement. Deeper tones can be easily reached using an electronic modifier designed by Zack.

When behaving naturally Gina is shy and reserved, moving in a similar fashion to Princess Diana when she first appeared in the media spotlight (not her later more groomed persona). She can lash out from this prissy personality slipping in and out of accents she has procured over her long espionage career.

Present Status

Gina has spent sixty years practising the art of subterfuge and infiltration. She has achieved the pinnacle of her profession and is able to inhabit a role with an astounding level of confidence within a very short time. She generally likes to have a few days to study a target if she is to impersonate them but can work in an improvisational way if required, and has on several occasions.

Gina is shy and unforthcoming even in meetings with her comrades whom she has known and trusted for over sixty-five years. She is confident enough, however, in her duties and abilities that she will embark upon a course of action, even a long infiltration mission, without asking for consent from or even informing her comrades.

Gina is still in love with Zack but has hidden it better than any of the various love-struck teenagers on the team. She tries to believe it is because her acting abilities are on an almost supernatural level but equally suspects that the relationships she has had to fake while undercover have helped her keep a certain distance from Zack.

Gina has no world-class reputation but her actions are celebrated by the international espionage community. Certain of Gina's missions are considered classic (some are even taught in infiltration lessons in the Spy Academy itself) without Gina ever having claimed credit for them. Gina considers anonymity the most precious of weapons and would not give it up for mere praise.

Gina shares a close friendship with Pegasus but does not share his fascination with the senior spies in the Council. She respects these agents for having survived a lifetime of espionage but even if they are legends only within the world of spying, fame is still the end of a spying career. Gina hopes to never attain the title "most famous spy in the world" as some have celebrated because that would be the most damning failure of her particular skills.

Behaviour

Gina in her rare natural state behaves in a reserved and almost submissive fashion. She crosses her legs, brings her elbows in to her waist and stares demurely at the floor. If antagonised then, rather than bring a heartfelt response to answer, she will adopt one of the many guises she has worn over the decades and bring retribution in their style.

She is an expert at many forms of martial arts and can recognise the moves of other professionals with ease. She can watch a fight between experts and be able to tell not only which martial art and which discipline was used but where they were likely to have trained. As though she were tasting wine and guessing the region and variety of grape, so can she accurately assess an aggressor's abilities.

Gina likes to be in every conversation between the teens in the team. She is the quietest of the team, however, enjoying the banter of the others; enjoying the feeling that she does not have to analyse every word. With her acting abilities Gina is either on or off, playing out or quiet. There is little middle ground. Although when quiet she is usually considered off-duty she is still recording mannerisms and details of her company. It is a skill she wishes she could switch off.

Writer's Guide

Gina is a feisty tomboy firecracker who kicks exactly as much butt as any of her male colleagues (and will accept a challenge to prove such a statement). She is persistent, relentless and pushy when pursuing a goal but in this, as with so much else, it is as though she is only playing the part of a diligent secret agent. It is the root of Gina's shy nervousness that she is forever playing a role. Whenever her acting ability is turned on she can be dramatic and dynamic, but when she has no façade to work with she shrinks into the background.

Gina would be the easiest character in The Spy Academy to short change in a story as she is so quiet unless provoked. She is very useful for exposition however as she can be already undercover in a place useful to the story when it begins or can remember useful information from a time she infiltrated a gang or organisation.

Like all the teens, Gina is an expert in her field and can recognise the exact skills of other hand-to-hand combatants. She is also the first of the team to recognise when somebody is lying (although the Jynx Elixir changes its subjects to such an extent that they cannot be read in such a way). She reads people with ease and can copy mannerisms, behaviour, accents and movements faultlessly.

Gina is deeply smitten with Zack but hides her feelings better than any of the team (due to her acting skills). She will often approach Zack for a gadget to assist her infiltration. These conversations should be played as painfully awkward flirting. She has the best relationship with Pegasus as she felt McCarthy was a surrogate father to her.

Her relatively pampered upbringing and enjoyment of family life (albeit a family that was torn from her and then was proved to be corrupt) gives her a sense of guilt she cannot shake. She is the least eager of the teens to learn about her true past. She has no idea of the politically proud conscientious objectors her parents were or their true fates. Rebel knows it all (from "The Parentage Document") but does not tell Gina because the rest of their story is too appalling.

She is not academically intelligent and has always fared badly at examinations. Despite this she has been a fast learner at everything to which she applies herself. Her memory has been greatly enhanced by the Jynx Elixir and she can recall complex and lengthy martial arts movements, for example, after a single viewing.

Gina will have had relationships with boys in her various undercover roles. They will have been few and short-lived but they have left their mark on Gina's personality. She feels guilty, of course, for having lied to the boys about her identity and embarrassed about her behaviour when in character. This intense awkwardness can be a way to make the teen audience sympathise with Gina's character. The feeling that everything is an act and that we can never behave naturally in front of people is a key phase of teenage life (that some of us never grow out of, in fact).

Gina is androgynous enough that she can play a male role for brief periods undercover. Make-up, padding and voice synthesisers from Zack make it possible for her to imitate a man but it should not happen too often (she is still exceptionally cute and shouldn't be made to seem masculine).

Gina in flashback must be handled carefully. Any time in the past that was spent undercover must be entered into the timeline so that other contributors can refer to it. Every month of infiltration spent means another few missions where Gina was unavailable and the team had to operate as a four-piece. The team should be fully manned whenever possible. An offhand comment "Gina spent a year infiltrating the organisation" means another $1/100^{th}$ of the twentieth century unavailable to her.

Ancient History

Ginechka was born in 1927 to a large family who had strong objections to the Stalinist regime but were wise enough to keep their opinions to themselves. When Ginechka was only eighteen months old, her parents refused to submit their eldest son for his tour of duty in the national armed service. The parents were imprisoned before they could complete their escape and the children were sent to different orphanages. Ginechka was sent to Chechnya where she won over a childless army General who rushed the adoption process.

Ginechka stayed in this home of opulence and comfort for ten years believing the General and his wife to be her real parents. When the General's wife became pregnant, Gina became a 5-yr-old elder sister to a pair of twin boys whom she adored. In 1939 she was brought by the General's wife to a decadent party for the families of the ruling class. Zander happened to be at the party and sent Kodie over to talk to the 12-yr-old girl. Ginechka was precociously displaying an ability to mimic any voice she heard which appeared to be perfect for Zander's upcoming project – the youth training project that would become the "Man of Steel" program. Her confident, assured manner at such a young age seemed to be an opportunity for Zander. He decided she must become a part of his project. Kodie's "interview" with the child confirmed his decision.

A few words to Stalin were all that was necessary to have Ginechka transferred to Zander's care. Ginechka was stolen from her family without the General's knowledge, the abduction blamed on foreign terrorists. Ginechka was informed that her family had been killed by dissidents. It was added that she had been adopted (something of which Ginechka was not aware) and that the adoption had not been properly processed. As such, her surname and status as a Soviet citizen had to be struck from official records. She was made a ward of state and Zander was made to appear her gracious benefactor and saviour.

She would now dedicate her life to the service of the Soviet state. Gina was given little time to grieve her loss and was whisked away to Moscow and the Lubyanka. Gina spent a year devoting her life to the Cheka training program. Here she was given specific training designed to mould her into the perfect infiltration agent. She eagerly absorbed all the knowledge to which she was exposed. Gina studied and replicated all the techniques shown to her including many recreated from crimes committed by Boris.

Zander returned on Gina's 13th birthday and offered her a place in the "Man of Steel" program as though it were a present to be accepted with gratitude. She was sweetly surprised by the arrival soon after of a young chess prodigy, Zacharov, who seemed to share with Gina a shyness that only evaporated in the expression of her natural abilities.

Gina had spent her life watching people closely so she could replicate them. In her years in the Pavlovian Institute and the Stalingrad bunker Gina watched Ivan Zander's movements with great interest. She noticed a great deal of duplicity in his words and actions and doubt began to grow in Gina's mind. Gina did not speak of her suspicions; she just monitored Zander and his close accomplices.

Boris seemed to act in a bizarre, almost unreadable way, as did Zander's assistant Kodie and Eagle, the security specialist. Gina noticed the same otherworldly affectations appearing in Zander in 1944. Early the following year the teens were given several courses of chemical elixirs. Gina noted that her behaviour and the behaviour of her comrades began to exhibit the same excesses. She urged her comrades to notice and curb these microscopic quirks but neglected to tell her superiors her findings.

Gina's conflicted feelings troubled her until Zacharov approached the team with his findings about the corrupt nature of Ivan Zander, the "Man of Steel" project and the entire Stalinist regime. Gina felt so proud of Zack at that moment that she accepted his conclusions without a hint of regret. She left the project that night bound for the West with doubts in her mind about her past and her very identity but the absolute conviction that she would spend the rest of her life with the boy who just saved it.

After the teens' first day with the Spy Academy, when they learned from Ivan Zander (now a defected entrepreneur) the truth of their immortality and abilities, Rebel made the decision to disallow personal relationships until their fight was won.
The Endless Fight

Gina spent the first three years in America studying the people and society first-hand and noting the colossal differences between realty and the perception she had experienced in the USSR: she did not try an undercover mission until 1949.

In 1954 Rhona noticed an emerging pattern in the street robberies in Manhattan and sent Gina undercover to investigate. Gina discovered a network of teenaged gangs pick-pocketing and thieving, all reporting back to the same Fagin-like master. When she realised this master criminal was Boris she successfully infiltrated the group. For three months she studied under Boris, worrying every day that her ruse might have been uncovered. When she eventually decided to close down the organisation Boris had anticipated the move and was gone.

In 1958 Gina disappeared while undercover in Vegas. Zander's operation had been threatening to spread west so Gina investigated in deep cover. While in the ranks of Zander's own employees, Gina saw Zack searching desperately through the casinos on the strip but did not dare to break cover. On her capture Eagle personally eliminated the poor family with whom Gina stayed and he cruelly told her the details of their deaths, blaming her for putting them in harm's way. Gina will never forgive Eagle for it. While she was captured Kodie pretended to "mistakenly" allow Gina a glimpse of a document (it was faked to draw the Spy Academy team into a trap months after the rescue). The teens were allowed to escape but Eagle tried to kill McCarthy, wounding him in the hip.

In 1968 Gina attempted to infiltrate a low-level New York street gang with links to Zander. When Eagle accompanied Kodie on a routine inspection of her gangs it was Eagle who detected the presence of another Jynx altered subject in the vicinity. In the ensuing chaos Gina's confidant was killed.

In 1971 Gina disappeared while attempting an infiltration of Zander's organisation. Gina remembers flashes of her time in captivity and knows she was treated with some brain-washing techniques by Kodie. She has never (to her knowledge) turned against her team but she fears there is mental conditioning dormant within her that may one day be activated.

In 1972 Gina was attacked by a black-suited martial artist while she slept. She sprang to life and defended herself, dodging shuriken, Sai blades and poison darts. As she defeated the first, three more poured into her hotel room. A total of twelve ninja assassins were fought off that night. After the event Gina realised that in her groggy state she had been using more than just her martial arts knowledge to defeat them; she had used her ability to watch, study and anticipate their moves.
In 1985 Rhona decided to send Gina on a deep cover mission to the New Falls community. The entire mission was populated with undercover allies, to encourage a restful three-month break for Gina. The concentration of operatives in New Falls drew an assassination/infiltration squad from Zander and a multinational terrorist consortium. Gina foiled the plan and captured most of the terrorists. Two of the terrorists were killed in the process.

In 1996 Gina entered Zander Tower during an offline upgrade of Cyber Lady's systems with the intention of copying and stealing memory files from the Cyber Lady database. She managed to bluff her way past the security staff and reach the memory banks on the thirtieth floor. Cyber Lady came back online unexpectedly and confronted Gina. Gina had to bluff that she had already reached the databanks and had inserted a magnetic explosive into them. Cyber Lady believed the lie and allowed her to escape.

In 1998 Gina again managed to infiltrate Zander Tower and reach Eagle's quarters unnoticed. She planted an explosive device that (according to Zack) would be capable of vaporising everything in the room. She made her escape confident and guiltless. Although such a method would usually be inexcusable for Gina she justified to herself that Eagle was technically dead already and she was merely completing nature's work. Rhona had learned of Gina's discussion with Zack and followed Gina to the tower. She managed to sneak into the building and circumvent security measures. She disabled the explosives more to spare Gina's conscience than to save Eagle, but has kept it secret from Gina.

The Future

Gina's family history is the most convoluted of any of the teens and has the most story potential. Her real parents were killed for no more than political objection and her siblings' descendants could be alive. If they are in possession of the knowledge that she was taken into a military family at the heart of the regime that killed their parents there could be reason for revenge. Gina was told that her adoptive family was killed but their true fates were never learned. Anything could have happened to them or their children (they could still be alive if they met Zander).

Gina has infiltrated so many organisations and become close to so many families while under another alias that there are hundreds of people left scattered through the twentieth century with reason to feel betrayed by Gina. Gina's undercover missions usually result in the target feeling aggrieved and angry at those who allowed themselves to be taken in. People have died in the past for the simple fact that they believed in Gina or accepted her stories. Those grieving family members left behind have reason to hate her.

Gina's love for Zack is a constant theme in The Spy Academy. If he is in danger she will suffer terrible worry and grief and vice versa. Although they will not be together until their fight is over (i.e. a final story is written) the chance of such a relationship is a powerful motivation.

Gina keeps secrets from her colleagues, not terrible secrets, merely the full details of her undercover experiences, too complex to be written and analysed. There will be many stories where Gina recalls some half-remembered conversation from a time undercover that informs their situation. Will she have to go undercover again to reprise the information? Will she remember another vital fact just a moment too late in a crucial mission?

Gina will pursue experts in martial arts to study and train under them or at the least fight alongside them. Gina has studied with assassins and tyrants and has guilty secrets from those times. She also made very interesting enemies.

Public Name   Boomer
True Name   Unknown
Occupation   Spy Academy Weapons Expert
Date of Birth   Circ. 1927
Apparent Age   18
Place of Birth   Russia
Height   6ft 1

Physical Appearance/Mannerisms

Boomer is tall, blonde and athletic with a sneering youthful disregard for almost everyone and everything. He views the world through slitted eyes, as though aiming at all he sees. Boomers mood goes through peaks and troughs of happiness and depression leading to moody behaviour typical of a true teenager.

Boomer's speech patterns are typically guarded and sarcastic. He will not reveal his opinions or emotions, preferring to offer only disdain and disinterest. Boomer is actually a man of strong feelings but his uncanny marksmanship has made him a terrifying weapon too deadly to allow himself to be manipulated. So it is that Boomer hides his feelings to almost everybody, leading to the sullen, cantankerous behaviour he so often displays.

Boomer has real love for his comrades in the Spy Academy but the enormity of the stakes for which they play make every aspect of their lives potentially crucial. There is no room for Boomer to enjoy something trivial, to relax and treat his gifts like a blessing.

More than any of the other teens he feels cursed. He has blood on his hands that he feels might never wash off.

Present Status

Boomer is a well-respected member of the Spy Academy, given authority and distance by every member. Even Pegasus knows to watch out for that hair-trigger temper of Boomer's and there have been many times that special allowances have been made for him that would be made for nobody else.

Boomer resents Zander for his condition like the rest of the teens but, unlike his comrades, he can find no redeeming factor to his gifts. An unwavering accuracy with virtually any projectile weapon has few uses other than bringing about death or injury. As technology accelerates and new and more complex weapons are created Boomer's ability keeps pace. He is able to operate each weapon he encounters with an unconscious talent. Only weapons with complicated computer systems are a stumbling block for Boomer (although these only slow him down rather than stop him). Zander has realised this and on occasions where he has acquired, contracted or designed a new weapon he has incorporated unnecessarily complex operating systems including dummy triggers and self-replicating codeword generators.

Boomer also feels a measure of responsibility for his specific gifts. He has been made aware of the action of the subconscious on the Jynx Elixir as it begins to mutate the body: he must have wished for these attributes.

Boomer is a sucker for Kodie. He still pines for her after sixty years even after every betrayal and manipulation he has suffered. Boomer believes that Kodie is suffering from multiple personality disorder (a valid assumption) and is convinced that Kodie's *true* personality is the warm, understanding girl he spoke to in the Stalingrad bunker, not the crazy, damaged lunatic that attacked them on the fields above it.

Boomer sees a happy ending waiting for him and Kodie that only requires him to believe in her. Unfortunately that means that he will fall for every trick she decides to try.

Behaviour

Boomer is the most typical teenager of the group. He is sullen, moody and prone to feeling sorry for himself (though he has more reason than most teens). Boomer will snap at any comment he might be able to interpret as an insult. He will spend long hours alone in his room writing in his journal (which he shows to no-one). Boomer will listen to very loud music and has had a room tunnelled specially for him to contain the acoustics.

Boomer no longer enjoys marksmanship but understands and performs his duty to assess and master every new weapon constructed. His records in the firing range are rarely broken. He makes his deadly disc device perform almost impossible acrobatic manoeuvres as it hunts out targets before exploding.

Boomer knows he is likely to fall for Kodie's manipulations whenever she attempts contact with him and has instructed his colleagues to watch his behaviour carefully. However he will always try to avoid his team-mates when responding to Kodie. He will say never again after each betrayal but cannot bring himself to follow his own advice.

Boomer will change his appearance to suit the times and will appear the most altered in flashback sequences. In the late sixties he grew his hair to shoulder length, in the seventies he had a shaggy, full haircut, in the eighties he had permanent stubble (Don Johnson, Miami Vice) and in the nineties he briefly had a short pony-tail. It was not that he was a fashion victim: it was more that trends allowed a more relaxed attitude to his personal grooming.

Boomer is friendly with all of his team-mates, even Pegasus, but it is Gina who understands him best. He will spend hours in her room talking about his problems leaving Zack to grow occasionally jealous of their relationship. It is the fact that their abilities are something of a curse to them that bonds them so closely together. She is asked to lie to everybody (even innocents) for long periods of time and he is asked to attack as though he were a weapon.

Writer's Guide

Boomer is the sullen, unresponsive typical teenager of the group. He is, and always has been, the least enthusiastic and most easily depressed of the teens. Writers must be careful not to cast him as "Kevin the teenager" (from Kevin and Perry) as he would become an easy target.

He would be a useful point of reference for readers of a similar type if written with a sympathetic ear. The depressive, moody, angst-ridden kids (surely that's most of them), Goths and Metal fans, and basically any person aged 10-20 who has had a bad day should be able to sympathise with, and look up to Boomer. If he comes across as whiny then it needs to be dialled down a notch or two.

Boomer's changing appearance through the decades should be remembered when writing flashbacks. There can be many changes and different styles but writers must be careful not to contradict other stories. If he has long hair in 1968 and 1970 then he should not have it all cut off for a story in 1969 for example.

In flashbacks Boomer is quite a different character. At the start of his career with the Spy Academy he was as enthusiastic as any of them but the relentless advances in weaponry, the fetishism of gun-culture in America and Boomer's own terrible mistake in 1971 have soured his feelings about espionage. The one weapon Boomer has been able to consistently enjoy is the boomerang. From the original "bent stick" design he first used on Eagle in 1945 (and which he occasionally uses today) to the three pointed signature weapon he first used in the late fifties, Boomer appreciates the non-lethality of the device. Although he has had many of them modified with sharp blades, explosive devices and electrical charges he has never used one to kill. He has a range of two, three and four pointed blades and knows how to modify them for non-return throwing (included in the design is a removable section that allows lift but prevents the circular path). The standard 3-blade design is not suitable for long distance throws but weighted two point designs can be flung an incredible distance by his Jynx-enhanced throwing arms.

Boomer will leave on solo missions from time-to-time but these are usually short term lasting no more than a few weeks. The one exception was the six month Vietnam mission of 1974.

Boomer will always perform the task of weapons specialist for the team, often using the specialised gadgets Zack will have designed for the mission. Boomer will always push Zack to design non-lethal devices.

Boomer's relationship with Kodie is one of the most important aspects of the character's life. His unrelenting faith in her true personality is a virtuous but simplistic trait of Boomers. Whether Kodie truly is the "good girl" personality that Boomer remembers or she is closer to the manipulative harridan shows to Zander is debatable. If she were ever to be cured of her multiple personality disorder it is likely that she would integrate her diverse characters into one new personality rather than *revert* to her *old* self. However if it were to happen (she would need to have the Elixir successfully removed from her system first) then perhaps she would become purely good or evil. Judgement on that decision will wait until such a story is eventually written. If the *last* Kodie story (or even if a temporary or imaginary cure is used) is of sufficient quality to demand an answer then it is open to that interpretation.

Boomer has a simplistic way of looking at the world. He does not appreciate tactics and planning the way Rebel and Rhona do, or understand the bigger picture in a comprehensive fashion as Zack can. He has the potential to understand complex issues and intellectual challenges but is unwilling to engage on that level. He sees himself as the Spy Academy's trigger and stubbornly refuses to put his heart and soul into his work. He thought he was doing the right thing in 1971 and his world fell apart.

Ancient History

Little is known about Boomer's birth beyond the fact that he was left at a Leningrad orphanage as a healthy six-month-old baby in the year 1928 with no notes or evidence to suggest from where he might have come. Boomer was assigned the name Josef but was never referred to as anything but *child* or *boy*. He was a moody child who was keenly aware that nobody wanted him, not even the orphanage staff who were forced to accept this extra burden. Josef refused to accept the name that he had been given when it was explained to him that he had been left, un-named, on the orphanage steps.

Josef tried to make friends in the rotating assembly of children coming in and out of the organisation, but the lack of stability pushed him to withdraw from society, retreating further into his own company. He once saw a bored guard spinning playing cards into his hat to pass the nightshift. Asking if he could join in the guard volunteered the deck to young Josef. Josef practised every night that his new friend was on duty and soon he became a precocious talent. He found he could skip stones across the river with far greater success than his friends in the orphanage. He was nick-named "Skip" to his great delight; a name he had earned for himself at last.

Skip practised with any projectile that came to hand and soon became a master of an kind of thrown object: ball, rock, paper plane, ball bearing etc. Between work detail Skip and the other children were given some education, and he found it easy enough. He soon found his talents being used to win bets for the guards. Skip tried to show off his talent when prospective parents arrived to choose a child but such a potentially destructive talent only warned away any possible parents.

In 1933 Skip was selected by the Cheka for training. Only aged six, the spies in the Cheka recognised that an ability such as his encouraged correctly could become invaluable to their forces. At the Lubyanka Skip met several other children of a similar age, including a very young Rhona.

Skip was thirteen when, in 1940, Rhona led him and a small team of students to investigate dissidents in the Moscow education system. The children found enough evidence but were trapped in a gymnasium as they tried to escape. Skip attacked their captors with a throwing hammer, successfully defeating them. Rhona was able to lead her team to safety, and Skip earned the new nickname "Hammer".

In 1941 *Hammer* and Rhona were relocated to the *"Man of Steel"* project run by Ivan Zander. It was there that Hammer met Kodie, a beautiful and sweet young research assistant who worked closely with the children. As he turned eighteen, Hammer experienced an overwhelming crush on the girl who seemed interested in him.

In very early 1945 the teens take the Jynx formula and report their experiences back to Kodie. She and Hammer spend long evenings talking about their lives and hopes for the future. Kodie and Hammer both had feelings of resentment and betrayal towards their real families: Hammer for his abandonment and Kodie for the abuse her father put her through. Hammer felt a deep bond forming with the scientist that he treasured.

When Zacharov approached the team with evidence of not only Stalin's corruption but Zander's terminal intentions towards the teens, he wanted Kodie to join their defection. Rhona, his oldest friend, was the one who expressed doubts about Kodie's trustworthiness. He felt a little betrayed by Rhona and decided to leave the group when they arrived in America; perhaps joining the US military. Confirmation of Rhona's suspicions came before they even left Stalingrad.

Hammer was utterly distraught, lacking identity and any place to put his trust. He found that place with his team in New York and followed Rebel into the Spy Academy. In his first battle in Manhattan the team discovered Zander newly entrenched as a defected businessman. Hammer tried every throwing weapon except the hammer.

The Endless Fight

In 1950 McCarthy and Rhona, tired of the loss of innocent life that their war had cost, conspired with Boomer to attempt a straight-forward assassination of Ivan Zander. Boomer had taken lives in the heat of combat but had never before considered the callous act of execution. Boomer allowed himself to be convinced by his team-mates and embarked upon the fatal mission. Rebel and Zack had just discovered the truth about "The Zander Protocols" when they learned that the attempt was in progress and raced to stop Boomer. They only managed to prevent the assassination by the slightest margin. Boomer knows how close he came to killing Zander and enacting the terrorist plans outlined in the Zander protocols.

In 1966 the team embarked upon a rescue mission to Sweden to save infants from Jynx experimentation. The team were captured by the

Elite squad in a nursery full of sleeping babies. Boomer was forced to deflect the aim of a newly-named Cyber Lady in order to allow their escape. The gunfire was deflected directly into Eagle's chest, bringing about his death, which was quickly reversed (in a horrific fashion) by Zander. Boomer cannot avoid feeling responsibility for Eagle's fate including his grotesque resurrection.

In 1971 evidence was uncovered of a conspiracy within the United States' government intent on spreading hostilities from Vietnam across Asia. Boomer was determined that such a pointless aggressive act not be allowed without proper democratic process. Boomer tried to use non-lethal means to apprehend the conspirators, shooting out a tyre to prevent an arrival at a meeting. The car crashed, killing both occupants. The evidence of conspiracy was later proven to be falsified and planted by Boris.

Immediately after that terrible mistake Boomer took 6 months leave from the Spy Academy and visited Vietnam. Eager to perform some action that was nothing but beneficial he devoted himself to freeing MIA POWs. While performing these acts of bravery he also prevented several civilian villages from abuse by US servicemen.

In 1977 Boomer let his Spy Academy duties slide for six months bringing about a confrontation between him and Rebel. Rebel accused Boomer of self-indulgence and laziness. Boomer did not offer any explanation, he simply led Rebel to the firing range. There they tested six newly delivered prototype firearms and Boomer scored a bulls-eye with each one. The realisation that he could now fire virtually any weapon with no training was such a blow to Boomer's sense of humanity that he had lost his way. Rebel offered support to his distraught friend.

In 1986 Boomer worked with a family who had escaped from Kodie's criminal network. Boomer was a bodyguard to them as they prepared to give evidence to the District Attorney about corruption in the New York legal system. As Boomer heard more stories about Kodie's gleeful cruelty to her colleagues his tender feelings for her began to sour. Boomer had to defend the family from an all-out assault by two dozen agents. He managed to gather enough evidence to implicate the DA and encourage his resignation.

By 1994 Boomer had begun to lose faith in Kodie's initial innocence. He had developed a relationship with a 20-yr-old graduate of the Academy who hoped for a long-term commitment from Boomer. In an infiltration mission to Zander Tower the entire team was captured. Kodie looked set to attempt torture and brain-washing techniques to discover what the team had witnessed when she had a sudden change of heart. She set Boomer free from his cell and shackles and, with a kiss, asked him to run. He managed to free the rest of the team who were doubtful as to Kodie's motives. Boomer refuses to believe that she was acting on Zander's orders to derail his personal life.

In 2001 Cyber Lady designed an artificial intelligence by herself - a daughter of sorts. She gave it a smaller version of her own drone body and an entire floor of memory space in the Zander Tower basement. On a reconnaissance mission from another tower block across the city Boomer saw a gap in security. He fired an explosive into the laboratory where the shell was housed and an electromagnetic pulsing device into the memory storage floor. The discharge disrupted communications for over an hour and wiped the AI. The personality attempted transmission to receiving stations but they had all been compromised. It effectively died.

The Future

Boomer's situation with Kodie is an obvious source for conflict. She feels possessive of Boomer and will attack anyone or anything that threatens her control of his emotional state. Any girl unfortunate enough to become a love interest for Boomer would be in terrible danger.

Boomer feels terrible guilt for what happened to Eagle. If Eagle were to regain lucidity, even for only a short period, he might remember what Boomer had done to him.

Boomer's hatred of Boris is something the master thief greatly enjoys. He takes enormous pleasure in tormenting the confused teen in whatever way a writer might imagine. Whole missions might be based upon an elaborate scenario designed by Boris in order to make Boomer cause the death of another innocent. The families of the two people killed in 1971 might return with the information that Boomer was responsible.

The escalation in power and accuracy of firearms is something of great concern to Boomer and great interest to many other parties. The ability to manipulate the legendary Boomer to work for them is a major goal for many espionage agencies and something Boomer must constantly be alert to avoid.

Boomer's habit of embarking from the Spy Academy with a solo mission in mind could bring trouble back for the entire group. His six months spent in Vietnam encountering corruption and abuse on both sides could bring stories of political dissident groups or criminal organisations that Boomer thwarted looking for revenge; or perhaps he needed a favour from a disreputable type that wants paying back. That portion of Boomer's life is, and should remain, a largely unexplored cathartic period when he reconciled that a soldier can be a good man even when his cause is less than noble. Only a small amount of flashback should be used in these stories to keep the period mysterious.

Boomer's origins are a mystery and open to any interpretation or manipulation by Zander and his forces.

Public Name	Pegasus
True Name	(Charles August McCarthy)
Occupation	Robotic facilitator
Date of Birth	Brought online (XX/XX/1964)
Apparent Age	Inapplicable
Place of Birth	New York
Height	3 ft
Weight	50 LB

Physical Appearance/Mannerisms

Pegasus is the floating robotic assistant and facilitator of the Spy Academy. He is an Artificial Intelligence and is completely aware of that fact and comfortable with it. Pegasus floats with the assistance of twin turbine propellers attached to his back. His head is a camera unit that moves as though it were on human shoulders. Pegasus has a number of spindly arms that fold out from and retract back into the torso but he uses the most human of these to gesture, point and wave. He has the same jerky, enthusiastic mannerisms of Chuck McCarthy, the man on whom his personality is based.

Chuck was a barrel-chested 5'9" muscular man with a cigar perpetually hanging from his mouth. He had dark hair in tight curls that turned salt and pepper grey in his mid-thirties and remained that way until he died. He had a crippling handshake, an explosive laugh and a tendency to say the wrong thing.

McCarthy would shrug in a comically exaggerated way when he felt that he was losing an argument. It is a specific gesture that has been programmed along with many others into Pegasus's database. All the teens save for Rebel look on Pegasus fondly as a remembrance of their deceased mentor. Rebel, who loved McCarthy as if he were his own father, has a harder time.

Present Status

The current model of Pegasus has remained the same externally for over a year and is set to become a classic. The shells (as they are known) contain constantly upgraded hardware with wireless connections to computer banks that update the software at a constant rate.

The limbs on the standard Pegasus model are all very weak, incapable of carrying or pushing, but there are many variations on this design. A "hard labour" shell with legs and powerful arms is used for some of the construction and repair work necessary around the Academy. There are miniaturised versions of the Pegasus shell that do nothing but send back reconnaissance to the base unit.

Pegasus's personality will not inhabit a humanoid model on a matter of principle. Although the Spy Academy is an espionage organisation Pegasus believes, as McCarthy did, that "eggs is eggs" and people shouldn't try to be what they are not.

Pegasus has a position of authority within the Spy Academy despite being an artificial personality. He outranks everybody on matters of Academy security. If he believes that any person may be a double agent or compromised in any way then, he has the authority to order their detention. This applies to the teens as well as any other agents or students. Only a Senior Council member may countermand his orders.

Pegasus is administrator for most of the activity of the Spy Academy. He monitors global politics and technology via the internet, world news organisations and Academy agents around the world. Pegasus collates information from United Nations sources and proposes which junior agents are to be invited to the Academy to learn from senior operatives. He also surveys general academic and sporting achievements in youth activities in order to find potential agents who will work for the Spy Academy itself in the long term once their training is complete. The final decisions are made by the Council.

Behaviour

Pegasus never leaves the Spy Academy's main cavern, constantly hovering around the organisation that has been the focus of his entire artificial life and much of his organic life as Chuck McCarthy. Pegasus never refers to himself as Chuck or McCarthy, acknowledging the distinct differences between the program and the man.

He floats around the team whenever they are in the cavern, recording as much conversation and discussion as possible for posterity. Many times the team have had to refer to Pegasus's backup recordings of meetings and briefings. Pegasus takes this duty to extremes at times, being basically nosey.

The robots personality is a slightly demented reminder of McCarthy that shares genuine relationships with the teens. Although Rebel is purposefully distant to Pegasus (he misses McCarthy too keenly to enjoy this pale reflection of the man) the others are close. Gina he sees as a surrogate daughter, Zack is like an antagonistic brother and Boomer shares with him the empty feeling of sometimes being no more than a weapon or tool to achieve a goal. Rhona is warm and supportive to Pegasus, but not in front of Rebel.

Pegasus spends as much time as possible with the members of the Senior Council (a rotating membership of retired secret agents from many nations). He behaves like an over-eager groupie desperate for an autograph and has clear favourites.

Pegasus spends what little downtime he has scouring the internet for progress in the world of robotics. He doesn't wish to be a passive patient in the process of his own evolution and helps Zack whenever possible. He also assists Rhona in her monitoring of ethical corporate business.

Pegasus is occasionally taken over by Zack who has secretly installed an access program into Pegasus's personality matrix. Zack will use Pegasus's voice and mannerisms with an electrical harness that controls his actions. Zack has only used this ability to ask awkward questions and sometimes to track guests in the Academy but still keeps it a secret.

Pegasus believes the gaps in his memory from these events are merely caused by a glitch in his voluminous programming.

Writer's Guide
Pegasus is not the shell that floats around the Spy Academy cavern all day, he is the program that drives it and provides the annoyingly sarcastic comments he so often says. The brain "or *soul*" of Pegasus is therefore in the massive computer banks hidden in every natural recess of the Spy Academy main cavern. It would be a disconcerting thing for a human being to know that their brain was being kept in a number of different rooms. The physical nature of his memory storage could be used to create a number of different stories based on lost/losing memories. See "Memento" and "The Eternal Sunshine of the Spotless Mind".

Pegasus, the robot (not android, droids are humanoid), is primarily a comedy character and one to sarcastically point out the absurdity of any stories before the reader does. He will be brash, boisterous and loud and occasionally foolish but it should be remembered that his personality is based on a man the teens greatly respected.

Pegasus is an everyman character who believed that the average working Joe is the most important person alive. He believes in America, democracy and justice and, in rare moments of clarity, is able to admit the flaws in all of these things. His character is that of an intelligent man who sometimes lets his passions override his mind.

It is a good idea when using Chuck McCarthy in flashbacks to show the similarities between him and the odd, floating technical wonder that now represents him. Don't forget also that there have been many different models of the Pegasus unit starting off in 1964 as a very basic unit and getting more and more technically advanced. On its arrival the first Pegasus unit had a scratchy, mechanical sounding voice box and smoking turbines prone to overheating. McCarthy also aged normally, so flashbacks to 1945 show him at 47, 1955 at 57 and 1963, when he died, at 65. The different ages of McCarthy and stages of development for Pegasus are an excellent way of marking time in flashbacks.

The months that the team spent without either McCarthy or Pegasus should be shown as a sad, empty time for the teens.

Zack's ability to override Pegasus's shell and leave only a gap in his memory is an interesting tool to explore the relationships of each of the teens but should be used sparingly. It is a breach of ethics for Zack to treat his comrade in this fashion plus there is only a limited number of reasons why Zack should need to do this.

Pegasus has several quirks with which a writer can lighten the mood:

– His nerdy fan-boy appreciation of the senior spies.

– His sarcastic irreverence to the teens' po-faced attitude.

– The old-fashioned expressions he often uses (like "Hill of Beans," "Eggs is Eggs," and "Doll-face".)

– Occasional moments of forgetfulness caused by programming glitches (use sparingly)

Pegasus can use a number of different shells when necessary and has many different arms and gadgets within his shell. Pegasus in his normal state acts as a kind of espionage Swiss-army knife. In his varied shells he can perform all sorts of other tasks.

Pegasus is a useful character in the event of an attack on the Spy Academy cavern. He will not succumb to gas or poison attacks; if his body is destroyed he will simply download into another shell. The only thing that would scare Pegasus is if the computer banks are threatened but this would not stop him from performing his duty.

Remember to always treat Pegasus as a character, not a machine. Zack designed an AI program complex enough that he did not need to write in directives for the personality to follow, but gave it instead McCarthy's opinions and judgement to help him always choose the right path. Pegasus is grateful to Zack for this freedom.

Ancient History

Charles McCarthy was born in 1899 to a large family of first generation Irish immigrants living in squalid accommodation in Hell's Kitchen in New York City. He was the eldest son, watching over his younger siblings as they grew and helping his mother and father run the drugstore over which they lived. McCarthy ran the lives of the other children while his parents worked towards the day when they could afford to buy the store and run it as their own business. He rarely attended school though insisted his siblings never missed a day. America entered the Great War in 1917 although he had already volunteered to serve his country.

The terrible things McCarthy witnessed in the years 1917 and 1918 would haunt him forever. He did not discuss his experiences with anybody and became increasingly upset with the way the American media swept away any mention of the War in the years that followed, vowing to do his best to prevent such things from happening in the future. He spent the following years being inducted into the Office of Strategic Services (a precursor to the CIA) and studied international politics. As the Great Depression hit in 1929 McCarthy's family struggled to hold on to their newly acquired business. McCarthy was too busy recording the rise of National Socialism in Germany to help his family. Although he sent most of his wages to his family McCarthy was too deep undercover in the German/American Nazi Bund movement to even contact them.

McCarthy spent the final years of the thirties undercover uncovering sponsors of the American Nazi movement. In 1940, when his leads had led to arrests of over 25 prominent agitators, McCarthy was able to return to help his family, but visited Washington often to protest about America's non-involvement in the Second World War. He would forever feel guilty about effectively abandoning them during the hardest years he could imagine.

After the Japanese attack on Pearl Harbor, McCarthy was relieved that America finally had the resolve to join the Allies against the Axis. Although he wished he could serve in the infantry once more (and redress some old concerns), he appreciated the importance of his role in military intelligence.

McCarthy was personally approached by President Roosevelt in 1942 with a job offer. An invitation to the White House turned into a meeting with the President and the British Prime Minister, Winston Churchill. They wanted a young American espionage agent of impeccable character to take stewardship of a long term venture the pair had initiated some years earlier. It was to be a place of international neutrality, a genuine new world order rising from the ashes of World War Two. With these words Roosevelt convinced McCarthy to dedicate his life to the project.

"If anything of worth is to come from these horrors we are forced to endure then it cannot be subject to the whims of publicity. The world has pulled together to fight evil but the world will divide again. If we are to keep the things we have learned and we are to keep on learning, then it must be done in secret."

It was McCarthy who suggested the name "The Spy Academy" and he was invited to be one of the original signatories on its charter. He asked that he be allowed to make a few additions to the final plans for the excavation of the caverns beneath Manhattan's subway and sewage systems. When he was given free reign to design as he felt necessary he asked FDR why he had been chosen over a higher ranking agent. FDR replied that rank was less important in such a covert organisation than trust. McCarthy had been given the highest praise, respect and glowing testimony from every agent they had approached.

McCarthy was not given the most senior position in the Spy Academy. The management of the organisation was given to a rotating council of senior covert agents of various nationalities. McCarthy was given the title facilitator and duties to spy on the Academy itself and ensure it remained incorruptible. He reported to no-one but his own conscience, though he suspected he was not the only fail-safe built into the organisation of The Spy Academy.

When the Stalingrad teens made their way through Germany they made contact with an American agent who gave them details to get in touch

118

with McCarthy. McCarthy researched the team and watched them closely as they met with five senior agents until he was convinced of their sincerity. He had agents waiting to assassinate the teens but eventually decided that he would simply trust them.

The Endless Fight 1 (McCarthy)

McCarthy mentored the teens as they settled into the American way of life. Their first few years were spent scouring the globe for possible Jynx Crystal s and foiling Zander's plans whenever they discovered them. He and Rebel both entered a Sicilian crime family in 1949 and set the foundations for nearly 60 years of infiltration and control. It was while they were undercover that Kodie established herself as boss of all New York crime families.

In 1950 McCarthy and Rhona conspired with Boomer to attempt a straight-forward assassination of Ivan Zander. Rebel and Zack had just discovered the truth about "The Zander Protocols" when they learned that the attempt was in progress and raced to stop Boomer.

McCarthy was personally responsible for the faked military secrets document that Boris procured for Zander in 1951. Zander relied on the falsified information contained therein for nearly a decade after the theft.

McCarthy was a devout capitalist and so in 1955 Boris stole property from his family home. In retaliation McCarthy designed an undercover mission to Moscow for the teens where Boris's reputation amongst the criminal underworld was ruined. Boris is still unable to return to his hometown and has no clue about the condition of his family.

In 1958 Gina was captured while undercover in Las Vegas. McCarthy felt a special bond to Gina who reminded him of his eldest daughter. Zack left the Academy to visit Vegas in a search for Gina and only discovered after the fact that she had been there. Zack begged McCarthy to authorise a retrieval mission which he did. The whole team stormed Zander's Vegas base and extracted Gina. In the escape McCarthy took a bullet in the hip which gave a swagger to his walk for the rest of his life. Gina called the bullet *Frank* because it made McCarthy resemble Sinatra when he walked.

The first Pegasus robot was constructed in 1959 based on plans designed by Zack. It was a functional, janitor unit used for repairing the generator units at temperatures beyond human tolerance.

McCarthy received a diagnosis of terminal cancer in 1962. He told only Zack who prepared an extensive series of questionnaires and tests to record his personality.

McCarthy's death in 1963 was in service to his country and the Spy Academy. He left behind a grieving but proud family. The "Option 12" documents that lured two Zander agents into a trap referred to a list of options Zack prepared for McCarthy when he learned his cancer was terminal. He initially rejected the first 12 plans but option 13 was "go home, retire, and let your family care for you these final few weeks". McCarthy thought about his family watching him die a painful death and asked, "What was Option 12 again?"

The Endless Fight 2 (Pegasus)

In 1964 Zack had collated the test results from McCarthy's various questionnaires and constructed a viable Artificial Intelligence. He inserted it into the computer banks beneath the Spy Academy cavern and used it to operate the Pegasus robotic shells. The interface soon allowed McCarthy's personality to return to the Academy albeit in an altered and sometimes crazy fashion.

By 1971 Gina disappeared while infiltrating Zander's organisation. Gina remembers being brainwashed by Kodie as she was held in Zander Tower. Pegasus gave analysis and assistance to the team as they infiltrated Zander's own organisation. Pegasus used small recon models to scout ahead for the group. All the models carried explosives which were used to destroy all the units and assist in the group's escape. On Gina's return Pegasus presented her with "Frank", the bullet retrieved from McCarthy's body. It had been left to Pegasus who had carried it in his shell ever since.

The in 1978 Pegasus met Eagle and had a bizarre chat. Pegasus was running on a single, low-memory unit, Eagle was isolated from his back-up. They shared a conversation over a cup of coffee at a diner. The waitress in attendence later required therapy and compensation from the government for the surreal encounter. Pegasus only remembers fleeting moments of the conversation as broadcast back to the Academy was patchy.

In 1989 Pegasus and Zack arranged the installation of an incredible offensive security system: wall-mounted guns, gas vents and a grid of hidden explosives. They were to be used in the event of an attack by enemy forces, but designed with Boris in mind. It turned out that Cyber Lady was the next one to gain access to the Academy and took control of the weapons. The systems have now been removed, but Pegasus has a few heavily armed vacant drones waiting around the cavern ready for activation in an emergency.

In 2000 Boris attempted to assassinate McCarthy's grandson, then 42. He survived after hours of surgery which Pegasus monitored through the hospital's computer system. As soon as the patient's condition stabilised Pegasus organised an aggressive mission to capture Boris but Zander promised to discipline him. He was eventually tried for the crime in 2002 but Zander manipulated the courts to set him free.

The Future

McCarthy had a long and exciting career in the American military and various espionage agencies before coming to the Spy Academy. His detailed reports are all a part of Pegasus's personality matrix. Any similarity of a modern case to one of his old ones could trigger suspicion in Pegasus. Perhaps an old foe (or descendant of such a villian) might come back to plague the world and only McCarthy knows how to beat him/her.

McCarthy influenced the creation of the Spy Academy itself. He added tunnels and access to the surface. He included extra rooms given to different teams of builders and committed only to memory. He may not have included the complete schematics when he helped construct

Pegasus. The cavern itself could prove to be a source of stories: hidden rooms, access used by persons unknown,

McCarthy's family lives on and have no idea about the existence of Pegasus. Pegasus is terrified that the world of the Spy Academy might spill over into his family's lives once more (it happened in 2000). Although Zander would frown upon such activity (Boris was punished for his attack) there are other enemies to the Spy Academy and many more for McCarthy himself.

Pegasus's personality is a huge, constantly evolving program but it is still subject to duplication or corruption. An aggressive virus inserted into his databanks might bring about a kind of Alzheimer's to the robot, requiring the team to find a cure before too much irreplaceable data is lost.

Pegasus can be accessed by Zack to talk to the other teens or track the movements of anybody Zack finds suspicious within the cavern. This has been done successfully for many years but it could get Zack or Pegasus into trouble. If a murder, for example, were to happen in the cavern witnessed by Zack through Pegasus's eyes how could Zack present his evidence without revealing his behaviour?

Pegasus might have specific parts of his memory erased by an untraceable program. He would suspect Zack at first but might find reason to suspect anybody. Piecing together the events he has lost would be an exciting way to structure an action/mystery story.

Observations

www.ingramcontent.com/pod-product-compliance
Lightning Source LLC
Chambersburg PA
CBHW071131250626
47159CB00006B/2201